LET'S ALL KILL CONSTANCE

LET'S ALL KILL CONSTANCE

A NOVEL

RAY BRADBURY

wm

WILLIAM MORROW
An Imprint of HarperCollins*Publishers*

HarperCollins books may be purchased for educational, business, or sales promotional use. For information please write: Special Markets Department, HarperCollins Publishers Inc., 10 East 53rd Street, New York, NY 10022.

FIRST EDITION

Designed by Bernard Klein

Printed on acid-free paper

Library of Congress Cataloging-in-Publication Data

Bradbury, Ray, 1920–
    Let's all kill Constance : a novel / by Ray Bradbury.— 1st ed.
    p. cm.
    ISBN 0-06-051584-8
    1. Private investigators—California—Los Angeles—Fiction. 2. Motion pictures actors and actresses—Fiction 3. Hollywood (Los Angeles, Calif.)— Fiction. 4. Aged women—Fiction. 5. Actresses—Fiction. I. Title.

PS3503.R167 L47 2003
813'.54—dc21

2002026416

03 04 05 06 07 JTC/RRD 10 9 8 7 6 5 4 3 2 1

This book is dedicated
with love
to my daughter
ALEXANDRA,
without whose help
the Third Millennium
might never have arrived.

and
again
with gratitude
and love
to
SID STEBEL

LET'S ALL KILL CONSTANCE

CHAPTER ONE

It was a dark and stormy night.

Is that one way to catch your reader?

Well, then, it was a stormy night with dark rain pouring in drenches on Venice, California, the sky shattered by lightning at midnight. It had rained from sunset going headlong toward dawn. No creature stirred in that downfall. The shades in the bungalows were drawn on faint blue glimmers where night owls deathwatched bad news or worse. The only thing that moved in all that flood ten miles south and ten miles north was Death. And someone running fast *ahead* of Death.

To bang on my paper-thin oceanfront bungalow door.

Shocking me, hunched at my typewriter, digging graves, my cure for insomnia. I was trapped in a tomb when the hammering hit my door, midstorm.

I flung the door wide to find: Constance Rattigan.

Or, as she was widely known, The Rattigan.

A series of flicker-flash lightning bolts cracked the sky and photographed, dark, light, light, dark, a dozen times: Rattigan.

Forty years of triumphs and disasters crammed in one brown surf-seal body. Golden tan, five feet two inches tall, here she comes, there she goes, swimming far out at sunset, bodysurfing back, they said, at dawn, to be beached at all hours, barking with the sea beasts half a mile out, or idling in her oceanside pool, a martini in each hand, stark naked to the sun. Or whiplashing down into her basement projection room to watch herself run, timeless, on the pale ceiling with Eric Von Stroheim, Jack Gilbert, or Rod La Rocque's ghosts, then abandoning her silent laughter on the cellar walls, vanishing in the surf again, a quick target that Time and Death could never catch.

Constance.

The Rattigan.

"My God, what are you doing *here?*" she cried, rain, or tears, on her wild suntanned face.

"My God," I said. "What are *you?*"

"Answer my question!"

"Maggie's east at a teachers' conference. I'm trying to finish my new novel. Our house, inland, is deserted. My old landlord said, your beach apartment's empty, come write, swim. And here I am. My God, Constance, get inside. You'll drown!"

"I already have. Stand back!"

But Constance did not move. For a long moment she stood shivering in the light of great sheets of lightning and the following sound of thunder. One moment I thought I saw the woman that I had known for years, larger than life, leaping into and jumping out of the sea, whose image I had witnessed on the ceiling and walls of her basement's projection room, backstroking through the lives of Von Stroheim and other silent ghosts.

Then, that changed. She stood in the doorway, diminished by light and sound. She shrank to a child, clutching a black bag to her chest, holding herself from the cold, eyes shut with some unguessed dread. It was hard for me to believe that Rattigan, the eternal film star, had come to visit in the midst of thunders.

I finally said again, "Come in, come in."

She repeated her whisper, "Stand back!"

She swarmed on me, and with one vacuum-suction kiss, harassed my tongue like saltwater taffy, and fled. Halfway across the room she thought to come back and buss my cheek lightly.

"Jeez, that's some flavor," she said. "But wait, I'm scared!"

Hugging her elbows, she sogged down to dampen my sofa. I brought a huge towel, pulled off her dress, and wrapped her.

"You do this to all your women?" she said, teeth chattering.

"Only on dark and stormy nights."

"I won't tell Maggie."

"Hold still, Rattigan, for God's sake."

"Men have said that all my life. Then they drive a stake through my heart."

"Are your teeth gritting because you're half-drowned or scared?"

"Let's see." She sank back, exhausted. "I ran all the way from my place. I knew you weren't here, it's been years since you left, but Christ, how great to find you! Save me!"

"From what, for God's sake?"

"Death."

"No one gets saved from that, Constance."

"Don't say that! I didn't come to die. I'm here, Christ, to live forever!"

"That's just a prayer, Constance, not reality."

"You're going to live forever. Your books!"

"Forty years, maybe."

"Don't knock forty years. I could use a few."

"You could use a drink. Sit still."

I brought out a half bottle of Cold Duck.

"Jesus! What's that?"

"I hate scotch and this is el cheapo writer's stuff. Drink."

"It's hemlock." She drank and grimaced. "Quick! Something else!"

In our midget bathroom I found a small flask of vodka, kept for nights when dawn was far off. Constance seized it.

"Come to Mama!"

She chugalugged.

"Easy, Constance."

"You don't have my death cramps."

She finished three more shots and handed me the flask, eyes shut.

"God is good."

She fell back on the pillows.

"You wanna hear about that damn thing that chased me down the shore?"

"Wait." I put the bottle of Cold Duck to my lips and drank. "Shoot."

"Well," she said. *"Death."*

CHAPTER TWO

I WAS beginning to wish there was more in that empty vodka flask. Shivering, I turned on the small gas heater in the hall, searched the kitchen, found a bottle of Ripple.

"Hell!" Rattigan cried. "That's hair tonic!" She drank and shivered. "Where was I?"

"Running fast."

"Yeah, but whatever I ran away from came with."

The front door knocked with wind.

I grabbed her hand until the knocking stopped.

Then she picked up her big black purse and handed over a small book, trembling.

"Here."

I read: *Los Angeles Telephone Directory, 1900.*

"Oh, Lord," I whispered.

"Tell me why I brought that?" she said.

I turned from the *A*s on down through the *G*s and *H*s and on through *M* and *N* and *O* to the end, the names, the names, from a lost year, the names, oh my God, the names.

"Let it sink in," said Constance.

I started up front. *A* for Alexander, Albert, and William. *B* for Burroughs. C for . . .

"Good grief," I whispered. "1900. This is 1960." I looked at Constance, pale under her eternal summer tan. "These people. Only a few are still alive." I stared at the names. "No use calling most of these numbers. This is—"

"What?"

"A Book of the Dead."

"Bull's-eye."

"A Book of the Dead," I said. "Egyptian. Fresh from the tomb."

"Fresh out." Constance waited.

"Someone sent this to you?" I said. "Was there a note?"

"There doesn't have to be a note, does there?"

I turned more pages. "No. Since practically everyone here is gone, the implication is—"

"*I'll* soon be silent."

"You'd be the last name in these pages of the dead?"

"Yep," said Constance.

I went to turn the heat up and shivered.

"What an awful thing to do."

"Awful."

"Telephone books," I murmured. "Maggie says I cry at them, but it all depends on *what* telephone books, *when*."

"All depends. Now . . ."

From her purse she pulled out a second small black book. "Open that."

I opened it and read, "Constance Rattigan" and her address on the beach, and turned to the first page. It was all *A*s.

"Abrams, Alexander, Alsop, Allen."

I went on.

"Baldwin, Bradley, Benson, Burton, Buss . . ."

And felt a coldness take my fingers.

"These are all *friends* of yours? I *know* those names."

"And . . . ?"

"Not all, but most of them, buried out at Forest Lawn. But dug up tonight. A graveyard book," I said.

"And worse than the one from 1900."

"Why?"

"I gave this one away years ago. To the Hollywood Helpers. I didn't have the heart to erase the names. The dead accumulated. A few live ones remained. But I gave the book away. Now it's back. Found it when I came in tonight from the surf."

"Jesus, you swim in this weather?"

"Rain or shine. And tonight I came back to find this lying like a tombstone in my yard."

"No note?"

"By saying nothing, it says everything."

"Christ." I took the old directory in one hand, Rattigan's small names and numbers book in the other.

"*Two* almost–Books of the Dead," I said.

"Almost, yes," said Constance. "Look here, and here, and also here."

She showed me three names on three pages, each with a red ink circle around it and a crucifix.

"These names?" I said. "Special?"

"Special, yes. *Not* dead. Or so I think. But they're marked, aren't they? With a cross by each, which means what?"

"Marked to die? Next up?"

"Yes, no, I don't know, except it scares me. Look."

Her name, up front, had a red ink circle around it, plus the crucifix.

"Book of the Dead, plus a list of the soon possibly dead?"

"Holding it, how does that book *feel* to you?"

"Cold," I said. "Awfully cold."

The rain beat on the roof.

"Who would *do* a thing like this to you, Constance? Name a few."

"Hell, ten thousand." She paused to add sums. "Would you believe nine hundred? Give or take a dozen."

"My God, that's too many suspects."

"Spread over thirty years? Sparse."

"Sparse!" I cried.

"They stood in lines on the beach."

"You didn't have to ask them in!"

"When they all shouted Rattigan!?"

"You didn't have to listen."

"What is this, a Baptist revival?"

"Sorry."

"Well." She took the last swig in the bottle and winced. "Will you help find this son of a bitch, or two sons of bitches, if the Books of the Dead were sent by separate creeps?"

"I'm no detective, Constance."

"How come I remember you half-drowned in the canal with that psycho Shrank?"

"Well . . ."

"How come I saw you up on Notre Dame at Fenix Studios with the Hunchback? Please help Mama."

"Let me sleep on it."

"No sleep tonight. Hug these old bones. *Now* . . ."

She stood up with the two Books of the Dead and walked across the room to open the door on black rain and the surf eating the shore, and aimed the books. "Wait!" I cried. "If I'm going to help, I'll need those!"

"Atta boy." She shut the door. "Bed and hugs? But no phys ed."

"I wasn't planning, Constance," I said.

CHAPTER THREE

AT two forty-five in the middle of the dark storm, a terrific lightning bolt rammed the earth behind my bungalow. Thunder erupted. Mice died in the walls.

Rattigan leaped upright in bed.

"Save me!" she yelled.

"Constance." I stared through the dark. "You talking to yourself, God, or me?"

"Whoever's listening!"

"We *all* are."

She lay in my arms.

The telephone rang at three A.M., the hour when all souls die if they need to die.

I lifted the receiver.

"Who's in bed with you?" Maggie asked from some country with no rains and no storms.

I searched Constance's suntanned face, with the white skull lost under her summer flesh.

"No one," I said.

And it was almost true.

CHAPTER FOUR

AT six in the morning dawn was out there somewhere, but you couldn't see it for the rain. Lightning still flashed and took pictures of the tide slamming the shore.

An incredibly big lightning bolt struck out in the street and I knew if I reached across the bed, the other side would be empty.

"Constance!"

The front door stood wide like a stage exit, with rain drumming the carpet, and the two phone books, large and small, dropped for me to find.

"Constance," I said in dismay, and looked around.

At least she put on her dress, I thought.

I telephoned her number. Silence.

I shrugged on my raincoat and trudged up the shoreline,

blinded by rain, and stood in front of her Arabian-fortress house, which was brightly lit inside and out.

But no shadows moved anywhere.

"Constance!" I yelled.

The lights stayed on and the silence with it.

A monstrous wave slammed the shore.

I looked for her footprints going out to the tide.

None.

Thank God, I thought. But then, the rain would have erased them.

"All right for you!" I yelled.

And went away.

CHAPTER FIVE

LATER I moved along the dusty path through the jungle trees and the wild azalea bushes carrying two six-packs. I knocked on Crumley's carved African front door and waited. I knocked again. Silence. I set one six-pack of beer against the door and backed off.

After eight or nine long breaths, the door opened just enough to let a nicotine-stained hand grab the beer and pull it in. The door shut.

"Crumley," I yelled. I ran up to the door.

"Go away," said a voice from inside.

"Crumley, it's the Crazy. Let me in!"

"No way," said Crumley's voice, liquid now, for he had opened the first beer. "Your wife called."

"Damn!" I whispered.

Crumley swallowed. "She said that every time she leaves

town, you fall off the pier in deep guano, or karate-chop a team of lesbian midgets."

"She *didn't* say that!"

"Look, Willie"—for Shakespeare—"I'm an old man and can't take those graveyard carousels and crocodile men snorkeling the canals at midnight. Drop that other six-pack. Thank God for your wife."

"Damn," I murmured.

"She said she'll come home early if you don't cease and desist."

"She *would,* too," I muttered.

"Nothing like a wife coming home early to spoil the chaos. Wait." He took a swallow. "You're okay, William, but no thanks."

I set the other six-pack down and put the 1900 telephone book and Rattigan's private phone book on top, and backed off.

After a long while that hand emerged again, touched Braille-wise over the books, knocked them off, and grabbed the beer. I waited. Finally the door reopened. The hand, curious, fumbled the books and snatched them in.

"Good!" I cried.

Good! I thought. In one hour, by God . . . he'll call!

CHAPTER SIX

IN one hour, Crumley called.

But didn't call me William.

He said, "Crud, crap, crapola. You really know how to hook a guy. What is it with these goddamn Books of the Dead?"

"Why do you say that?"

"Hell, I was born in a mortuary, raised in a graveyard, matriculated in the Valley of the Kings outside Karnak in upper, or was it lower, Egypt? Some nights I dream I'm wrapped in creosote. Who *wouldn't* know a book that's dead when it's served with his beer?"

"Same old Crumley," I said.

"I wish it wasn't. When I hang up I'm calling your wife!"

"Don't!"

"Why not?"

"Because—" I stopped, gasped, and then blurted out, "I need you!"

"Crud."

"Did you hear what I said?"

"I heard," he muttered. "Christ."

And at last, "Meet you down by Rattigan's. Around sunset. When things come out of the surf to get you."

"Rattigan's."

He hung up before I could.

CHAPTER SEVEN

EVERYTHING by night, that's the ticket. Nothing at noon; the sun is too bright, the shadows wait. The sky burns so nothing dares move. There is no fun in sunlit exposure. Midnight brings fun when the shadows under trees lift their skirts and glide. Wind arrives. Leaves fall. Footsteps echo. Beams and floorboards creak. Dust sifts from tombstone angel wings. Shadows soar like ravens. Before dawn, the streetlights die, the town goes briefly blind.

It is then that all good mysteries start, all adventures linger. Dawn never was. Everyone holds their breath to bind the darkness, save the terror, nail the shadows.

So it was only proper that as dark waves were striking a darker shore, I met Crumley on the sand, out front of her big white Arabian-fortress beach house. We walked up and looked in.

All the doors still stood wide, bright lights burned inside while Gershwin punched holes in a player-piano roll in 1928 to be played again and again, triple time, with no one listening except me and Crumley walking through lots of music, but no Constance.

I opened my mouth to apologize for calling Crumley.

"Drink your gin and shut up." Crumley thrust a beer at me.

"Now," he went on, "what the hell does all this mean?" He thumbed the pages of Rattigan's personal Book of the Dead. "Here, here, and over here."

There were red ink marks circling a half-dozen names, with deeply indented crucifixes freshly inscribed.

"Constance guessed, and so did I, that those marks meant the owners of those names were still alive, but maybe not for long. What do you think?"

"I don't," said Crumley. "This is your picnic. I was all set to head for Yosemite this weekend, and you show up like a film producer who improves the flavor of screenplays by peeing on every other scene. I'd better run for Yosemite right now; you got that look of a wild rabbit with intuitions."

"Hold on." For he was starting to move. "Don't you want to prove or disprove which of these names are still kicking or which dropped dead?"

I grabbed the book, then tossed it back so he had to catch. It fell open at one page with a more-than-enormous crucifix by an almost-circus-banner name. Crumley scowled. I read the name upside down: Califia. Queen Califia. Bunker Hill. No address. But there was a phone number.

Crumley could not take his eyes off it, scowling.

"Know where that is?" I said.

"Bunker Hill, hell, I know, I know. I was born a few blocks north of there. A real free-for-all stewpot of Mexicans, Gypsies, stovepipe-out-the-window Irish, white trash and black. Used to go by there to look in at Callahan and Ortega, Funeral Directors. Hoped to see real bodies. My God, Callahan and Ortega, what names, right there in the middle of Juarez II, Guadalajara bums, dead flowers from Rosarita Beach, Dublin whores. Crud!" Crumley suddenly yelled, furious at listening to his own travel talk, half selling himself on my next expedition. "Did you hear me? Did you listen? God!"

"I heard," I said. "So why don't we just call one of those red circle numbers to see what's aboveground or below?"

And before he could protest, I seized the book and ran up the dune to Rattigan's outdoor pool, brightly lit, with an extension phone on a glass-top patio table, waiting. I didn't dare look at Crumley, who had not moved as I dialed.

A voice answered from long miles away. That number was no longer in service. Damn, I thought, and then, Wait!

I dialed information swiftly, got a number, dialed it, and held the phone out so Crumley could hear the voice:

"Callahan and Ortega, good evening," the voice said, a full rich ripe brogue from center stage of Abbey Theatre. I smiled wildly. I saw Crumley, below, twitch.

"Callahan and Ortega," the voice repeated, louder now, its temper roused. A long pause. I stayed mum. "Who the hell is this?"

I hung up before Crumley reached me.

"Son of a bitch," he said, hooked.

"Two blocks, maybe three, from where you were born?"

"Four, you conniving bastard."

"Well?" I said.

Crumley grabbed Rattigan's book.

"Almost but not quite a Book of the Dead?" he said.

"Want to try another number?" I opened the book, turned, and stopped under the *R*s. "Here's one, oh Lord yes, even better than Queen Califia."

Crumley squinted. "Rattigan, Mount Lowe. What kind of Rattigan lives up on Mount Lowe? That's where the big red trolley that's been dead half my lifetime used to take thousands up for picnics."

Memory shadowed Crumley's face.

I touched another name.

"Rattigan. St. Vibiana's Cathedral."

"What kind of Rattigan, holy jumping Jesus, hides out in St. Vibiana's Cathedral?"

"Spoken like a born-again Catholic." I studied Crumley's now-permanent scowl. "Want to know? I'm on my way."

I took three false steps before Crumley swore. "How the hell you going to get there with no license and no car?"

I kept my back turned. "You're going to take me."

There was a long brooding silence.

"Right?" I prompted.

"You know how in hell to find where the Mount Lowe trolley once ran?"

"I was carried up by my folks when I was eighteen months old."

"That means you can show the way?"

"Total recall."

"Shut up," said Crumley as he tossed a half-dozen bottles of beer into the jalopy. "Get in the car."

We got in, left Gershwin to punch piano-roll holes in Paris, and drove away.

"Don't say anything," said Crumley. "Just nod your head left, right, or straight ahead."

CHAPTER EIGHT

"I'LL be damned if I know why in hell I'm doing this," Crumley muttered, almost driving on the wrong side of the street. "I said, I'll be damned if I know why in hell—"

"I heard you," I said, watching the mountains and the foothills coming closer.

"You know who you remind me of?" Crumley snorted. "My first and only wife, who knew how to flimflam me with her shapes and sizes and big smiles."

"Do *I* flimflam you?"

"Say you don't and I'll throw you out of the car. When you see me coming, you sit and pretend to be working a crossword puzzle. You're maybe four words into it before I grab your pencil and shove you outta the way."

"Did I ever do *that*, Crumley?"

"Don't get me mad. You watching the street signs? Do so.

Now. Tell me, why are you heading this damn-fool expedition?"

I looked at the Rattigan phone book in my lap. "She was running away, she said. From Death, from one of the names in this book. Maybe one of them sent it to her as a spoiled gift. Or maybe she was running *toward* them, like we're doing, heading for one to see if he's the sinner who dared to send tombstone dictionaries to impressionable child actresses."

"Rattigan's no child," Crumley groused.

"She is. She wouldn't've been so great up on the screen if she hadn't kept one heckuva lot of her Meglin Kiddie self locked up in all those sexual acrobatics. It's not the old Rattigan who's scared here; it's the schoolgirl in panic running through the dark forest, Hollywood, full of monsters."

"You whipping up another of your Christmas fruitcakes full of nuts?"

"Does it sound like it?"

"No comment. Why would one of these red-lined friends send her two books full of lousy memories?"

"Why not? Constance loved a lot of people in her time. So, years later, one way or another, a lot of people hate her. They got rejected, left behind, forgotten. She got famous. They were found with the trash by the side of the road. Or maybe they're real old now and dying, and before they go they want to spoil things."

"You're beginning to sound like me," Crumley said.

"God help me, I hope not. I mean—"

"It's okay. You'll never be Crumley, just like I'll never be Jules Verne Junior. Where in hell are we?"

I glanced up quickly.

"Hey!" I said. "This is it. Mount Lowe! Where the great old red trolley train fell down dead, a long time ago.

"Professor Lowe," I said, reading some offhand memory from the dark side of my eyelids, "was the man who invented balloon photography during the Civil War."

"Where did *that* come from?" Crumley exclaimed.

"It just came," I said, unsettled.

"You're full of useless information."

"Oh, I don't know," I said, offended. "We're here at Mount Lowe, right? And it's named for Professor Lowe and his Toonerville Trolley scaling its heights, right?"

"Yeah, yeah, sure," Crumley said.

"Well then, Professor Lowe invented hot-air balloon photography that helped catch enemy images in the great war of the states. Balloons, and a new invention, trains, won for the North."

"Okay, okay," Crumley grumbled. "I'm outta the car and ready to climb."

I leaned out the car window and looked at the long weed-choked path that went up and up a long incline in evening's gathering shadows.

I shut my eyes and recited. "It's three miles to the top. You really want to walk?"

Crumley glared at the foothill.

"Hell, no." He got back in the car and banged the door shut. "Is there any chance we could run off the edge of that damn narrow path? We'd be goners."

"Always the chance. Onward!"

Crumley edged our jalopy to the foot of the mostly blind path, cut the engine, got out, walked over, kicked some dirt, and pulled some weeds.

"Hallelujah!" he exclaimed. "Iron, steel! The old rail track, didn't bother to yank it out, just buried it!"

"See?!" I said.

His face crimson, Crumley plunged back in, almost submerging the car.

"Okay, smart-ass! Damn car won't start!"

"Put your foot on the starter!"

"Damn!" Crumley stomped the floorboard. The car shimmied.

"Double-damn smart-ass kids!"

We ascended.

CHAPTER NINE

THE way up the mountain was a double wilderness. The dry season had come early and burned the wild grass to sere crispness. In the rapidly fading light the whole hillside up to the peak was the color of wheat, fried by the sun. As we rode, it crackled. Two weeks before, someone had tossed a match and the whole foothill had exploded in flame. It was head-lined in the papers and lit the television news, the flames were so pretty. But now the fire was gone and the chars and dryness with it. There was a dead-fire smell as Crumley and I threaded the lost path winding up Mount Lowe.

On the way, Crumley said, "It's good you can't see over my side. A thousand-foot drop."

I clutched my knees.

Crumley noticed. "Well, maybe only a five-hundred-foot drop."

I shut my eyes and recited off my clenched eyelids.

"The Mount Lowe railway was part electric, part cable car."

Crumley, made curious, said, "And?"

I unclenched my knees.

"The railway opened July Fourth, 1893, with free cake and ice cream and thousands of riders. The Pasadena City Brass Band rode the first car playing 'Hail, Columbia.' But considering their passage into the clouds, they had shifted to 'Nearer My God to Thee,' which made at least ten thousand people along the way cry. Later in the ascension they decided to do 'Upward, Always Upward' as they reached the heights. They were followed in three cable cars by the Los Angeles Symphony; the violins in one car, the brass in a second, and the timpani and woodwinds in the third car. In the confusion, the conductor was left behind with his baton. Later in the day the Salt Lake City Mormon Tabernacle Choir ascended, also in three cars; sopranos in one, the baritones in another, and the bass in the third. They sang 'Onward, Christian Soldiers,' which seemed very appropriate as they vanished in the mist. It was reported that ten thousand miles of red, white, and blue bunting covered all of the trolleys and the trains and the cable cars. When the day was finally over, one semihysterical woman who admired Professor Lowe for what he had done to bring about the creation of the Mount Lowe railway and its taverns and hotels was quoted as saying, 'Praise God from whom all blessings flow and also praise Professor Lowe,' which made everyone cry again," I babbled on.

Crumley said, "I'll be damned."

I added, "The Pacific Electric Railway ran to Mount Lowe, the Pasadena Ostrich Farm, Seleg Lion Zoo, San Gabriel Mission, Monrovia, Baldwin's Ranch, and Whittier."

Crumley mumbled under his breath and drove on in silence.

Taking that as a hint, I said, "Are we there yet?"

"Cowardly custard," said Crumley. "Open your eyes."

I opened my eyes.

"I think we're there."

And we were. For there stood the ruins of the old rail station, and beyond that, a few charred struts of the burned pavilion.

I got out slowly and stood with Crumley surveying miles of land that went forever to the sea.

"Cortés never saw better," said Crumley. "View's great. Makes you wonder why they didn't rebuild."

"Politics."

"Always is. Now, where in hell do we find someone named Rattigan in a place like this?"

"*There!*"

Some eighty feet away, behind a huge spread of pepper trees, was a small cottage half-sunk in the earth. Fire hadn't touched it, but rain had worn its paint and battered its roof.

"There's got to be a body in there," Crumley said as we walked toward it.

"Isn't there always a body, or else why come see?"

"Go check. I'll stand here hating myself for not bringing more booze."

"Some detective." I ambled over to the cottage and had

one helluva time yanking its door wide. When it finally whined and gave way, I lurched back, afraid, and peered in.

"Crumley," I said at last.

"Yeah?" he said, sixty feet away.

"Come see."

"A body?" he said.

"Even *better*," I said in awe.

CHAPTER TEN

WE entered a labyrinth of newsprint. A labyrinth; hell, a catacomb with narrow passages between stacks of old newspapers—the *New York Times,* the *Chicago Tribune,* the *Seattle News,* the *Detroit Free Press.* Five feet on the left, six on the right, and a pathway between which you might jockey through, fearful of avalanches that could crush and kill.

"Holy magoly!" I breathed.

"You can say that again," Crumley groused. "Christ, there must be ten thousand Sunday and daily papers stacked here, in layers—look, yellow down below, white on top. And not just one stack, ten dozen—my God, a hundred!"

For indeed the catacomb of newsprint hollowed back through twilight shadow to curve out of sight.

It was a moment, I later said, like Lord Carnarvon opening Tut's tomb in 1922. All those ancient headlines, those obituary piles, that led to what? More news stacks and more beyond. Crumley and I sidled through with hardly enough space for bellies or behinds.

"God," I whispered, "if ever a *real* earthquake hit—"

"It did!" came a voice from far down the stacked tunnel of print. A mummy cried. "Kicked the stacks! Almost pancaked me!"

"Who's there?" I called. "Where in hell *are* you?"

"A great maze, yeah?" The mummy's voice yelled in glee. "Built it myself! Morning extra by night final, race specials, Sunday comics, you name it! Forty years! A museum library of news, un–fit to print. Keep moving! Around the bend to your left. I'm here somewhere!"

"Move!" Crumley panted. "There's gotta be a space with fresh air!"

"That's it!" the dry voice called. "You're close. Bear left. Don't smoke! Damn place's a firetrap of headlines: 'Hitler Takes Power,' 'Mussolini Bombs Ethiopia for Kindling,' 'Roosevelt Dead,' 'Churchill Builds Iron Curtain,' swell, huh?"

We turned a final corner among tall flapjack stacks of print to find a clearing in the forest.

On the far side of the clearing was an army cot. On the cot lay what seemed a long bundle of beef jerky or a mummy rampant from the earth. There was a strong smell. Not dead, I thought, not alive.

I approached the cot slowly, with Crumley behind. I knew the odor now. Not death, but the great unwashed.

The rag bundle stirred. Some ancient blanket shreds

flaked from a face like watermarks on mud shallows. A faint crack of light glinted between two withered lids.

"Pardon my not rising," the withered mouth trembled. "Chez Monsieur from Armentières, haven't got up in forty years." It cackled a cackle that almost killed it. It began to cough.

"No, no, I'm okay," it whispered. The head fell back.

"Where the hell you been?"

"Where . . . ?"

"I been expecting you!" said the mummy. "What year is it? 1932? 1946? 1950?"

"You're getting warmer."

"1960. Howzat?"

"Bull's-eye," said Crumley.

"I'm not all crackers." The old man's dry dust mouth quavered. "You bring my vittles?"

"Vittles?"

"No, no, couldn't be. It's a kid, totes the dog food through that Grub Street newsprint alley, can by can, or the whole damn thing falls. You're not him—or he?"

We glanced behind and shook our heads.

"How you like my penthouse? Original meaning: place where they used to pent up people so they couldn't run amok. We gave it a different meaning and raised the rent. Where was I? Oh, yeah. How you like this joint?"

"A Christian Science reading room," said Crumley.

"Darn tootin'," said Ramses II. "Started 1925. Couldn't stop. Smash and grab, not much smash, mainly grab. It all started one day when I forgot to throw out the morning papers. Next thing there was a week collected and then more *Tribune/Times/Daily News* trash. That there on your right is 1939. On the left: 1940. One stack back: '41. Neat!"

"What happens if you want a special date and it's four feet down?"

"I try not to figure that. Name a date."

"April ninth, 1937," leaped off my tongue.

"Why the hell *that?*" said Crumley.

"Don't stop the boy," came the whisper from under the dust blanket. " 'Jean Harlow, dead at twenty-six. Uremic poisoning. Services mañana. Forest Lawn. Nelson Eddy, Jeanette MacDonald duet at the obsequies.' "

"My God!" I exploded.

"Pretty damn smart, huh? More!"

"May third, 1942," popped from my mouth.

" 'Carole Lombard killed. Air crash. Gable weeps.' "

Crumley turned to me. "Is that *all* you know? Dead film stars?"

"Don't fret the kid," said the old voice six feet under. "What you doing here?"

"We came—" said Crumley.

"It's about—" I said.

"Don't." The old man whirled a dust storm of thoughts. "You're a *sequel!*"

"Sequel?"

"Last time anyone climbed Mount Lowe looking to jump off, he failed, went back down, and was hit by a car that cured his living. Last time someone really came was . . . noon today!"

"Today!?"

"Why not? Come find the old crock, drowned in dust, no rolls in the hay since '32. Someone *did* come a few hours ago, shouted down those tunnels of bad news. Recall that fairy tale porridge mill? Say 'go!' it made hot porridge. Kid got it started. Forgot the 'stop' word. Damn porridge flooded the whole town. People ate their way door-to-door. So I got newsprint, not porridge. What did I just say?"

"Someone shouted down—"

"The corridor between the *London Times* and *Le Figaro?* Yeah. Woman, braying like a mule. Yells emptied my bladder. Threatened to tiddlywink my stacks. One shove and it's dominoes, she screamed, whole damn print architecture *squashes* me!"

"I should think earthquakes—"

"Had 'em! Shook the hell out of 'Yang-Tse River Deluge' and 'Il Duce Conquers,' but here I am. Even the big one, in '32, didn't kick my poker stacks. Anyway, this wild woman screamed all my vices and demanded certain papers from special years. I said try first row on the left, then the right; I keep all the raw stuff high. I heard her wrestle the stacks. Her cursing could have set 'London on Fire!' She slammed the door, skedaddled, looking for a place to jump. I don't think a car got her. Know who she was? I been holding out on you. Guess?"

"I can't," I said, stunned.

"See that desk there in cat litter? Scrap the litter, lift the stuff with fancy type."

I stepped to the desk. Under a tangle of sawdust and what

seemed to be bird droppings, I found two dozen identical invitations.

" 'Clarence Rattigan and—' " I paused.

"Read it!" said the old man.

" 'Constance Rattigan,' " I gasped, and went on. " 'Are pleased to announce their marriage atop Mount Lowe, June tenth, 1932, at three in the afternoon. Motor and rail escorts. Champagne following.' "

"That hit you where you live?" said Clarence Rattigan.

I glanced up.

"Clarence Rattigan and Constance Rattigan," I said. "Hold on. Shouldn't Constance's maiden name be listed?"

"Looks like incest, you mean?"

"Strange peculiar."

"You don't get it," the lips husked. "Constance made me change *my* name! It *was* Overholt. She said she was damned if she'd give up her first-class moniker for a second-rate hand-me-down, so—"

"You got baptized before the ceremony?" I guessed.

"Never was but finally did. Episcopal deacon down in Hollywood thought I was nuts. You ever try to argue with Constance?"

"I—"

"Won't take yes for an answer! 'Love Me or Leave Me,' she sang. I liked the tune. Hit me with the baptismal oil, laid on the unction. First damn fool in America to burn his birth certificate."

"I'll be damned," I said.

"No. *Me*. What you staring at?"

"You."

"Yeah, I know," he said. "I don't seem like much. Wasn't much then. See that bright doohickey on top o' the invites? Mount Lowe train motorman's brass handle. Rattigan liked the way I banged that brass. Me, the motorman on the Mount Lowe trolley! Jesus! Is there any beer anywhere?" he added suddenly.

I gathered my spit. "You claim you were Rattigan's first husband and then ask for beer?"

"I didn't say I was her first husband, just one of some. Where's that beer?" The old man gummed his lips.

Crumley sighed and pulled some stuff from his pockets. "Here's beer and Mallomars."

"Mallomars!" The old man stuck out his tongue and I placed one on it. He let it melt on his tongue like a Jesus wafer. "Mallomars! Women! Can't live without 'em!"

He half sat up for beer.

"Rattigan," I urged.

"Oh, yeah. Marriage. She rode up on the trolley and went wild with the weather, thought it was my creation, proposed, and after our honeymoon, one night, found out I had nothing to do with the climate, grew icicles, and vamoosed. My body will never be the same." The old man shivered.

"Is that all?"

"What d'ya mean, *all?! You* ever throw her two falls out of three?"

"Almost," I whispered.

I pulled out Rattigan's phone book. "This clued us onto you."

The old man peered at his name circled in red ink. "Why would someone send you here?" He mused over another swallow. "Wait! You some sort of *writer?*"

"Some sort."

"Well hell, that's *it!* How long you known her?"

"A few years."

"A year with Rattigan's a thousand and one nights. Lost in the Fun House. Hell, son. I bet she red-circled my name because she wants you to write her autobiography. Starting with me, Old Faithful."

"No," I said.

"She ask you to take notes?"

"Never."

"Damn, wouldn't that be great? Anyone ever written a book wilder than Constance, more wrathful than Rattigan? A bestseller! Lie down with Rattigan, get up with sequined fleas. Run down the hill, sign a publisher! I get royalties for revelations! Okay?"

"Royalties."

"Now gimme another Mallomar, more beer. You still need more guff?"

I nodded.

"That other table . . ." An orange crate. "A list of wedding guests."

I went to the orange crate and riffled through some bills until I found one piece of quality paper and peered at it as he said, "You ever wonder where the name California came from?"

"What's that—"

"Pipe down. The Hispanics, when they marched north from Mexico in 1509, carried books. One published in Spain had an Amazon queen ruling in a land of milk and honey. Queen Califia. The country she ruled was named California. The Spaniards took one look down this here valley, saw the milk, ate the honey, and named it all—"

"California?"

"So, check that guest list."

I looked and read: "Califia! My God! We tried to call her today! Where is she now?"

"That's what the Rattigan wanted to know. It was Califia predicted our predestined marriage, but not our downfall. So Rattigan trapped me with a hammerlock and mobbed this place with bums and bad champagne, all because of Califia. 'Where the hell is she?' she shouted today, down the tunnel of newsprint. '*You* would know!' she yelled. 'Not guilty!' I yelled back up the tunnel. 'Go, Constance! Califia ruined us both. Go kill her, then kill her again. Califia!'"

The mummy fell back, exhausted.

"You said *all* that," I asked. "At noon today?"

"Some such," sighed the old man. "I sent Rattigan off for blood. I hope she finds that damned half-ass-trologer and . . ." His voice wandered. "More Mallomars?"

I laid the cookie on his tongue. It melted. He talked fast.

"You wouldn't think it to see this boneless wonder, but I got half a mil in the bank. Go see. I mouth-to-mouth-breathed Wall Street stocks not dead, just asleep. From 1941 through Hiroshima, Enewetak, and Nixon. I said buy IBM, buy Bell. Now I got this great spread with a view overlook-

ing L.A., a one-holer Andy Gump behind, and the Glendale
Market, well tipped, sends up a kid with Spam, canned
chili, and bottled water! The life of Riley! You guys done
shadowboxing my past?"

"Almost."

"Rattigan, Rattigan," the old man went on. "Good for a
few hoots and raucous applause. She was written up in those
papers from time to time. Grab one paper off the top of
each stack, four on the right, six on the left, all different. She
left snail-track spoors on the path to Marrakech. Today she
came back to clean her catbox."

"Did you actually see her?"

"Didn't need to. That yell would split Rumpelstiltskin
and sew him back up."

"Is that all she wanted, Califia's address?"

"And the papers! Take 'em and go to hell. It's been a long
divorce with no surcease."

"Can I have this?" I lifted an invitation.

"Take a dozen! Only ones showed up were Rattigan's
Kleenex guys. She used to wad and throw 'em over her shoul-
der. 'You can always order more,' she said. Grab the invites.
Steal the newsprint. What did you say your name was?"

"I didn't."

"Thank God! Out!" said Clarence Rattigan.

Crumley and I threaded our way, gingerly, through the
labyrinthine towers, borrowed copies of eight different
newspapers from eight different stacks, and were about to
head out the front door when a kid with a loaded box barred
our way.

"What you got there?" I said.

"Groceries."

"Mostly booze?"

"Groceries," the kid said. "He still in there?"

"Don't come back!" King Tut's voice cried from deep down far away in the newsprint catacomb. "I won't be here!"

"He's there, all right," said the kid, two shades paler.

"Three fires and an earthquake! One more ahead! I feel it coming!" The mummy's voice faded.

The kid looked at us.

"It's all yours." I stepped back.

"Don't move, don't breathe." The kid put one foot inside the door.

Crumley and I didn't move, didn't breathe.

And he was gone.

CHAPTER ELEVEN

CRUMLEY managed to swerve his wreck around and head us back downhill without falling off the edge. On the way, my eyes brimmed.

"Don't say it." Crumley avoided my face. "I don't want to hear."

I swallowed hard. "Three fires and an earthquake. And more coming!"

"That did it!" Crumley hit the brakes. "Don't *say* what you think, dammit. Sure, another quake's coming: Rattigan! She'll rip us all! Out, out, and walk!"

"I'm afraid of heights."

"Okay! Zip your lip!"

We drove down beneath twenty thousand leagues of silence. Out on the street, in traffic, I scanned the newspapers, one by one.

"Hell," I said, "I wonder why he let us have these?"

"Whatta you see?"

"Nothing. Zero. Zilch."

"Gimme." Crumley grabbed and used one eye on the news, one on the road. It was starting to rain.

" 'Emily Starr, dead at twenty-five,' " he read.

"Watch it!" I cried as the car drifted.

He scanned another paper. " 'Corinne Kelly divorces Von Sternberg.' "

He hurled the paper over his shoulder.

" 'Rebecca Standish in hospital. Fading fast.' "

Another toss, another paper. " 'Genevieve Carlos marries Goldwyn's son.' So?"

I handed him three more between flashes of rain. They all went into the backseat.

"He said he wasn't crackers. Well?"

I shuffled the news. "We're missing something. He wouldn't keep these for the hell of it."

"No? Nuts collect peaches, plums collect nuts. Fruit salad."

"Why would Constance—" I stopped. "Hold on."

"I'm holding." Crumley clenched the wheel.

"Inside, society page. Big picture. Constance, good Lord, twenty years younger, and the mummy, that guy up there, younger, with more flesh, not bad looking, their wedding, and on one side Louis B. Mayer's assistant, Marty Krebs, and on the other, Carlotta Q. Califia, noted astrologer!"

"Who told Constance to marry up on Mount Lowe. Astrologer forecasts, Constance takes the dive. Find the obituary page."

"Obit—?"

"Find it! Whatta you see?"

"Holy cow! The daily horoscope and the name—Queen Califia!"

"What's the forecast? Fair? Mild? Good day to start a garden or marry a sucker? Read it!"

" 'Happy week, happy day. Accept all proposals, large or small.' So, what's next?"

"We *got* to find Califia."

"Why?"

"Don't forget—she's got a red circle around her name, too. We got to see her before something awful happens. That red crucifix means death and burial. Yes?"

"No," said Crumley. "Old Tutankhamen up on Mount Lowe is still flopping around, and his name's red-inked, too, with a crucifix!"

"But he feels someone's coming to get him."

"Who, Constance? That knee-high wonder?"

"All right, the old man's alive. But that doesn't mean Califia hasn't already been wiped out. Old Rattigan didn't give us much. Maybe she can give us more. All we need is an address."

"That's *all*? Hey." Crumley suddenly swerved to the curb and got out. "Most people never think, Constance didn't think, we didn't think. One place we never looked. The Yellow Pages! What a goof! The Yellow Pages!"

He was across the sidewalk and into a public phone booth to scrabble through some beat-up Yellow Pages, tear out a page, and tote it back. "Old phone number, useless. But maybe a half-ass address."

He shoved the page in my face. I read: QUEEN CALIFIA. *Palmistry. Phrenology. Astrology. Egyptian Necrology. Your life is mine. Welcome.*

And the damned zodiac street locale.

"So!" said Crumley, as close to hyperventilation as he ever got. "Constance tipped us to the Egyptian relic and the relic names Califia who said marry the beast!"

"We don't know that!"

"Like hell we don't. Let's see."

He put the car in gear and we went fast, to see.

CHAPTER TWELVE

WE drove up near Queen Califia's Psychic Research Lodge, dead center of Bunker Hill. Crumley gave it a sour eye. Then I nodded to one side and he saw what to him was a lovely sight: CALLAHAN AND ORTEGA FUNERAL PARLOR.

That raised his spirits. "It's like a homecoming," he admitted.

Our jalopy stopped. I got out.

"You coming in?" I said.

Crumley sat staring out the windshield, hands on the steering wheel, as if we were still moving. "How come," he said, "everything seems downhill with us?"

"You coming in? I *need* you."

"Outta the way."

He was halfway up the steep concrete steps and then the cracked cement walk before he stopped, surveyed the big white dilapidated bird cage of a house, and said, "Looks like the half bakery where they bake your misfortune cookies."

We continued up the walk. On the way we met a cat, a white goat, and a peacock. The peacock flirted its thousand eyes, watching us pass. We made it to the front door. When I knocked, an unseasonable blizzard of paint snowflakes rained on my shoes.

"If that's what holds this joint up, it won't be long," observed Crumley.

I rapped on the door with my knuckles. Inside I heard what sounded like a massive portable safe being trundled across a hardwood floor. Something heavy was shoved up against the other side of the door.

I raised my hand again, but a high sparrow voice inside cried, "Go away!"

"I just want—"

"Go away!"

"Five minutes," I said. "Four, two, one, for God's sake. I need your help."

"No," the voice shrilled, "I need *yours.*"

My mind spun like a Rolodex. I heard the mummy. I echoed him.

"You ever wonder where the name California came from?" I said.

Silence. The high voice lowered to almost a whisper. "Damn."

Three sets of locks rattled.

"Nobody knows that about California. *Nobody.*"

The door opened a few inches.

"Okay, give," the voice said.

A hand like a great plump starfish thrust out.

"Put it there!"

I put my hand in hers.

"Turn it over."

I turned it, palm up.

Her hand seized it.

"Calmness."

Her hand massaged mine; her thumb circumnavigated the lines on my palm.

"Can't be," she whispered.

More quiet motions as she thumbed the pads under my fingers.

"*Is,*" she sighed.

And then, "You remember being born!"

"How did you know *that?*"

"You must be the seventh son of a seventh son!"

"No," I said, "just me, no brothers."

"My God." Her hand jumped in mine. "You're going to live forever!"

"No one does."

"*You* will. Not your body. But what you *do*. What do you do?"

"I thought my life was in your hands."

She let out a breathless laugh.

"Jesus. An actor? No. Shakespeare's bastard son."

"He had no sons."

"Melville, then. Herman Melville's by-blow."

"Wish it were true."

"Is."

I heard the great weight behind the door roll back on creaking wheels. The portal drifted wide.

I saw an immense woman in an immense crimson velvet queen's robe receding on roller wheels in a metal throne across the hardwood floor to the far side of the room. She stopped by a table on which rested not one, but four crystal balls, coruscant with light from a green-and-amber Tiffany lamp. Queen Califia, astrologer, palmist, phrenologist, past and futurist, sank inside three hundred mountainous pounds of too-too-solid flesh, her stare flashing X rays. A vast iron safe hulked in the shadows.

"I don't bite."

I stepped in. Crumley followed.

"But leave the door open," she added.

I heard the peacock scream in the yard and dared to hold out my other hand.

Queen Califia reared back as if burned.

"You know Greene, the novelist?" she gasped. "Graham Greene?"

I nodded.

"Wrote about a priest who lost faith. Then witnessed a miracle he himself had caused. The shock at his renewed faith almost killed him."

"So?"

"So." She stared at my hand as if it were disconnected from my arm. "Lord."

"Is it happening to you?" I said. "What happened to that priest?"

"Oh, God!"

"Did you lose your faith, your power to heal?"

"Yes," she murmured.

"And now, just now, it all came back?"

"Dammit! Yes!"

I crushed my hand to my chest to blind it.

"How'd you guess that?" I said.

"No guess. Scares the hell out of me."

She saw the wedding invitation and the newspaper in my outstretched hand.

"You've been up to see *him*," she said.

"You looked. That's cheating."

That brought a half smile and then a snort. "People ricochet off him and end up here."

"Not often enough, I think. May I sit?" I said. "I'll fall if I don't."

She nodded at a chair a few feet away, a safe distance. I fell into it.

Crumley, ignored, looked peevish.

"You were saying?" I said. "People don't visit old Rattigan often. No one knows he's alive on Mount Lowe. But someone went there and yelled at him today."

"She yelled?" The great mountain almost melted in remembrance. "*I* wouldn't let *her* in."

"Her?"

"It's always a mistake"—Queen Califia cast a glance

toward the crystal balls—"to guess futures and, damn fool, *tell* them. I give hints, not facts. I won't tell people what stocks to buy, what flesh to borrow. Diets, yes, I sell vitamins, Chinese herbs, but not longevity."

"You just did."

"You're different." She leaned. The rollers under her massive chair squealed.

"The future lies ahead of you. I've never seen a future so clear. But you are in terrible danger. I see all the time that you have to live, but someone could destroy it. Be careful!"

She paused for a long moment, closed her eyes, and then said, "You her friend? You know who I mean."

I said, "Yes—and no."

"Everyone says that. She's black and white and wild all over."

"Who are we talking about?"

"We don't need names. I wouldn't let her in. An hour ago."

I looked at Crumley. "We're catching up, getting close."

"Don't," said Califia. "The way she yelled I thought she might have a knife. 'I'll never forgive you!' she screamed. 'You gave us the wrong road maps, down instead of up, lost instead of found. May you roast in hell!' Then I heard her drive away. I won't sleep at all tonight."

"Did she say—this sounds crazy—where she was going?"

"Not crazy at all," said Califia. "I would think that since she went first to that old fool on Mount Lowe who she dropped after one bad night, then me who put her up to it, well, next, why not the poor sap who performed the ceremony? She wants to get us all together, to push us off a cliff!"

"She wouldn't do that."

"How would *you* know? How many women you had in your life?"

At last I said, sheepishly, "One."

Queen Califia mopped her face with a handkerchief big enough to cover half her bosom, regained her composure, and slowly advanced on me, propelling herself on glider wheels with dainty pushes of her incredibly small shoes. I could not take my eyes off how tiny her feet were compared with the vast territory above, and the great lunar face that loomed on that expanse. I saw the ghost of Constance drowned beneath that flesh. Queen Califia shut her eyes.

"She's using you. You love her?"

"Carefully."

"Keep your clothes on and your motor running. She ask you to get her with child?"

"Not in so many words."

"No words, just bastard stillborns. She whelped monsters down the whole L.A. basin, lousy Hollywood Boulevard, dead-end Main. Burn her bed, scatter the ashes, call a priest."

"Which priest, where?"

"I'll put you in touch. Now . . ." She paused, refusing to spit out the name. "Our friend. She's always missing. One of her dodges, to make men panic. One hour with her does it. They riot in the streets. You know the game Uncle Wiggily? Well, Uncle Wiggily says jump back ten hops, head for the Hen House, *quit!*"

"But she *needs* me!"

"No. She dines on spoilage. Blessed are the wicked who relish wickedness. Your bones will knead her bread. If she were here, I'd run her down with my chair. God, she made Rome's ruins. Hell," she added. "Let me see your palm again." Her massive chair creaked. Her wall of flesh threatened.

"You going to take back what you saw in my hand?"

"No. I just say what I see in an open palm. You will have another life beyond this! Tear up that newspaper. Burn the wedding invitation. Leave town. Tell her to die. But tell her cross-country by phone. Now, out!"

"Where do I go from here?"

"God forgive me." She shut her eyes and whispered, "Check that wedding invitation."

I raised the invite and stared.

"Seamus Brian Joseph Rattigan, St. Vibiana's Cathedral, celebrant."

"Go tell 'im his sister is in two kinds of hell, and to send holy water. Scram! I got lots to do."

"Like what?"

"Throw up," she said.

I clutched Father Seamus Brian Joseph Rattigan in my sweaty palm, backed off, and bumped into Crumley.

"Who are *you?*" said Califia, finally noticing my shadow.

"I thought you knew," Crumley said.

We went out and shut the door.

The whole house shifted with her weight.

"Warn her," Califia cried. "Tell her, don't come back."

I looked at Crumley. "She didn't tell *your* future!"

"Thank the Lord," said Crumley, "for small blessings."

CHAPTER THIRTEEN

BACK down the steep cement steps we went, and under the pale moonlight by the car, Crumley peered into my face. "What's that mad-dog look?"

"I've just joined a church!"

"Get in, for Christ's sake!"

I got in, running a fever.

"Where to?"

"St. Vibiana's Cathedral."

"Holy mackerel!"

He banged the starter.

"No." I exhaled. "I couldn't stand another face-on. Home, James, a shower, three beers, and to bed. We'll catch Constance at dawn."

We passed Callahan and Ortega, nice and slow. Crumley looked almost happy.

Before the shower, the beers, and the snooze, I pasted seven or eight newsprint front pages on the wall over my bed, where I might wake in the night in hopes of solutions.

All the names, all the pictures, all the headlines big and small saved for mysterious or not mysterious reasons.

Behind me, Crumley snorted. "Horse apples! You going to commune with news that was dead as soon as it was printed?"

"By dawn, sure, they just might drop off the wall, slide under my eyelids, and get stuck in the creative adhesive in my brain."

"Creative adhesive! Japanese *bushido!* American bull! Once those things are off the wall, like you, do they propagate?"

"Why not? If you don't put in, you never get out."

"Wait while I kill this." Crumley drank. "Lie down with porcupines, get up with pandas?" He nodded at all those pictures, names, and lives. "Constance in there somewhere?"

"Hidden."

"Hit the shower. I'll stand guard on the obituaries. If they move, I'll yell. How does a margarita strike you as night-cap?"

"I thought you'd never ask," I said.

CHAPTER FOURTEEN

St. Vibiana's Cathedral awaited us. Downtown L.A. Skid Row. At noon, heading east, we stayed off the main boulevards.

"Ever seen W. C. Fields in *If I Had a Million?* Bought some old tin lizzies and rammed road hogs. Super," said Crumley. "That's why I hate highways. I want to roadkill. You listening?"

"Rattigan," I said. "I thought I knew her."

"Hell." Crumley laughed gently. "You don't know anyone. You'll never write the great American novel, because you don't know shoats from shinola. You overestimate character where there is none, so you upchuck fairy princes, virgin milkmaids. Most writers can't even do that, so you go with your taffy pulls, thirteen to the dozen. Let those realists scoop dog doo."

I remained silent.

"Know what your problem is?" Crumley barked, and then softened his voice. "You love people not worth loving."

"Like you, Crum?"

He glanced over cautiously.

"Oh, I'm okay," he admitted. "I've more holes than a sieve, but I haven't fallen through. Hold on!" Crumley hit the brakes. "The pope's home away from home!"

I looked out at St. Vibiana's Cathedral in the midst of the slow-motion desolation of long-dead Skid Row.

"Jesus," I said, "would have built here. You coming in?"

"Hellfires, no! I was kicked outta confession, age twelve, when I skinned my knees on wild women."

"Will you ever take Communion again?"

"When I die. Hop out, buster. From Queen Califia to the Queen of Angels."

I climbed out.

"Say a Hail Mary for me," Crumley said.

CHAPTER FIFTEEN

INSIDE the cathedral it was empty, just after noon, and just one penitent was waiting by the confessional when a priest arrived and beckoned her in.

His face confirmed I was in the right place.

When the woman left, I ducked in the other side of the confessional, tongue-tied.

A shadow moved in the lattice window.

"Well, my son?"

"Forgive me, Father," I blurted out. "Califia."

The other confessional door banged wide with a curse. I opened my door. The priest reared as if I had shot him.

It was Rattigan Déjà Vu. Not svelte in ninety-five pounds of suntanned seal-brown flesh, but marrowed in a wire-coat-hanger skeleton-thin Florentine Renaissance priest. Constance's bones hid there, but the flesh skinned over the bones was skull pale, the priest's lips were ravenous for salvation, not bed and sinful breakfasts. Here was Savonarola begging God to forgive his wild perorations, and God silent, with Constance's ghost burning from his eyes, and peering from his skull.

Father Rattigan, riven, found me harmless save for that word, jerked his head toward the vestry, led me in, and shut the door.

"You *her* friend?"

"No, sir."

"Good!" He caught himself. "Sit. You have five minutes. The cardinal is waiting."

"You had better go."

"Five minutes," said Constance from inside the mask of this genetic twin. "Well?"

"I've just visited—"

"Califia." Father Rattigan exhaled with controlled despair. "The Queen. Sends people she can't help. She has her church, not mine."

"Constance has disappeared again, Father."

"Again?"

"That's what the Queen, ah, Califia said."

I held out the Book of the Dead. Father Rattigan turned its pages.

"Where'd you get this?"

"Constance. She said someone sent it to her. To scare her, maybe, or hurt her, or God knows what. I mean, only she knows if it's a real threat."

"You think she might just be hiding to spoil things for

everyone?" He deliberated. "I myself am of two minds. But then there were those who burned Savonarola *then* and elevate him *now*. A most peculiar sinner-cum-saint."

"Aren't there similarities, Father?" I dared to say. "Lots of sinners became saints, yes?"

"What do you know about Florence in 1492 when Savonarola made Botticelli burn his paintings?"

"It's the *only* age I know, sir, Father. Then Savonarola, now Constance . . ."

"If Savonarola knew her, he'd kill himself. No, no, let me think. I've starved since dawn. Here's bread and wine. Let's have some before I fall."

The good father pulled a loaf and a jug out of the vestry closet, and we sat. Father Rattigan broke the bread, then poured a small wine for himself, and a large for me, which I took gladly.

"Baptist?" he said.

"How did you guess?"

"I'd rather not say."

I tipped back my glass. "Can you help me with Constance, Father?"

"No. Oh, Lord, Lord, maybe."

He refilled my glass.

"Last night. Can it *be?* I stayed in the confessional late. I felt . . . as if I were waiting for someone. Finally, near midnight, a woman entered the confessional and for a long while was silent. Finally, like Jesus calling Lazarus, I insisted, and she wept. It all came out. Sins by the pound and the truckload, sins from last year, ten years, thirty years past, she couldn't stop, on and on, night on dreadful night, on and on, and finally she was still and I was about to instruct her with Hail Marys when I heard her running. I checked the other side of the confessional but only smelled perfume. Oh Lord, Lord."

"Your sister's scent?"

"Constance?" Father Rattigan sank back. "Hell burned twice, that perfume."

Last night, I thought. So close. If Crumley and I had only come then.

"You'd better go, Father," I said.

"The cardinal will wait."

"Well," I said, "if she returns, would you call me?"

"No," said the priest. "The confessional's as private as a lawyer's office. Are you that upset?"

"Yes." I twisted the wedding ring on my finger, absently. Father Rattigan noticed.

"Does your wife know all this?"

"Approximately."

"That sounds like delicatessen morality."

"My wife trusts me."

"Wives do that, God bless them. Does my sister seem worth saving?"

"Doesn't she to *you?*"

"Dear God, I gave up when she claimed mouth-to-mouth resuscitation was a Kama Sutra pose."

"Constance! Still, Father, if she shows up again, could you call my number and hang up? I'd know you were signaling her arrival."

"You do know how to split hairs. Give me your number. I see in you not so much a Baptist but a fair Christian."

I gave him my number as well as Crumley's.

"Just one ring, Father."

The priest studied the numbers. "We all live on the slope. But some, by a miracle, grow roots. Don't wait. Your phone may never ring. But I'll give your number to my assistant, Betty Kelly, too, just in case. Why are you doing this?"

"She was heading fast off a cliff."

"Watch out she doesn't take you with. I'm ashamed I said that. But as a child she skated out and stopped in mid-traffic to laugh."

He fixed me with a bright needle eye. "But why do I tell you this?"

"It's my face."

"Your *what?*"

"My face. I look in mirrors but never catch myself. The expression always changes before I can trap it. It's got to be a blend of the Boy Jesus and Genghis Khan. It drives my friends crazy."

This relaxed some of the priest's bones. "Does *idiot savant* sound right?"

"Almost. The school bullies took one look and beat the hell out of me. You were saying?"

"Was I? Yes, well, if that screaming woman was Constance, and her voice seemed different, she gave me orders. Imagine, orders to a priest! Gave me a deadline. Said she'd be back in twenty-four hours. I must give complete forgiveness for all her sins, twenty thousand strong. As if I could

assign such mass-market absolution. I told her she must forgive herself, and ask others for forgiveness. God loves you.
'But He *doesn't*,' she said. And then she was gone."

"*Will* she come back?"

"With doves on her shoulders or lightning bolts."

Father Rattigan walked me to the front of the cathedral.
"And how does she look? Like a siren singing to lure
damned sailors to drown. Are you a poor damn sailor?"

"No, just someone who writes people on Mars, Father."

"I hope they are happier than we are. Wait! Good Lord,
there *was* a thing she said. That she was joining a new
church. And might not come back to douse my ears."

"What church, Father?"

"Chinese. Chinese and Grauman's. Some *church*!"

"To many it is. You've been there?"

"To see *King of Kings,* I found the forecourt superior to
the film. You look as if you're about to break and run."

"To the new church, Father. Chinese. Grauman's."

"Stay off the quicksand footprints. Many sinners have
sunk there. What film's playing?"

"Abbott and Costello in *Jack and the Beanstalk.*"

"Lamentable."

"Lamentable." I ran.

"Mind the *quicksand*!" Father Rattigan called after me as
I raced out the doors.

CHAPTER SIXTEEN

ON the way across town I was a hot-air balloon full of Great Expectations. Crumley kept hitting my elbow to make me calm down, calm down. But we *had* to get to that other church.

"Church!" Crumley muttered. "Since when do double features sideline the Father, Son, and Holy Ghost?"

"*King Kong!* That's when! 1932! Fay Wray kissed my cheek."

"Holy mackerel." Crumley switched on the car radio.

"—afternoon—" a voice said. "Mount Lowe—"

"Listen!" I said, my stomach a chunk of ice.

The voice said, "Death . . . police . . . Clarence Rattigan . . . victim . . ." A flare of static. "Freak accident . . . victim smothered, smothered . . . old newspapers. Recall brothers in Bronx? Saved stacks of old papers that fell and killed the brothers? Newspapers . . ."

"Turn it off."

Crumley turned it off.

"That poor lost soul," I said.

"Was he really *that* lost?"

"Lost as you can get without giving it the old heave-ho."

"You want to drive by?"

"Drive by," I said at last, making noises.

"You didn't know him," said Crumley. "Why those noises?"

The last police car was leaving. The morgue van had long since left. A lone policeman on his motorcycle stood at the bottom of Mount Lowe. Crumley leaned out his window.

"Anything to keep us from driving up?"

"Just me," said the officer. "But I'm leaving."

"Were there any reporters?"

"No, it wasn't worth it."

"Yeah," I said, and made more noises.

"Okay, okay," Crumley groused, "wait till I get this damn car aimed before you upchuck your hairball."

I waited and fell apart, silently.

The motorcycle policeman left, and it was a long late afternoon journey up to the ruined temple of Karnak, the destroyed Valley of the Kings, and lost Cairo, or so I said along the way.

"Lord Carnarvon dug up a king, we bury one. I wouldn't mind a grave like this."

"Bull Montana," said Crumley. "He was a wrestling cowboy. Bull."

At the top of the hill there were no ruins, just a vast pyramid of newspapers being rummaged by a bulldozer driven by an illiterate. The guy bucking the wheeled machine had no idea he was reaping Hearst's outcries, '29, or McCormick's eruptions in the *Chicago Tribune, '32.* Roosevelt, Hitler, Baby Rose Marie, Marie Dressler, Aimee Semple McPherson, one, twice buried, forever shy. I cursed.

Crumley had to restrain me from leaping out to seize VICTORY IN EUROPE or HITLER DEAD IN BUNKER or AIMEE WALKS FROM SEA.

"Easy!" Crumley muttered.

"But look what he's doing to all that priceless stuff! Let go, dammit!"

I leaped forward to grab two or three front pages.

Roosevelt was elected on one, dead on another, reelected on the third, and then there was Pearl Harbor and Hiroshima at dawn.

"Jesus," I whispered, pressing the damned lovely things to my ribs.

Crumley picked up "I WILL RETURN," SAYS MACARTHUR. "I get your point," he admitted. "He was a bastard, but the best emperor Japan ever had."

The guy minding the grim reaping machine had stopped and was eyeing us like more trash.

Crumley and I jumped back. He plowed through toward a truck already heaped with MUSSOLINI BOMBS ETHIOPIA, JEANETTE MACDONALD MARRIES, AL JOLSON DEAD.

"Fire hazard!" he yelled.

I watched a half-hundred years of time pour into the Dumpster.

"Dry grass and newsprint, firetraps," I mused. "My God, my God, what if—"

"What if what?"

"In some future date people use newspapers, or books, to *start* fires?"

"They already do," said Crumley. "Winter mornings, my dad shoved newspaper under the coal in our stove and struck a match."

"Okay, but what about *books?*"

"No damn fool would use a book to start a fire. Wait. You got that look says you're about to write a ten-ton encyclopedia."

"No," I said. "Maybe a story with a hero who smells of kerosene."

"Some hero."

We walked over a killing field of littered days, nights, years, half a century. The papers crunched like cereal underfoot.

"Jericho," I said.

"Someone bring a trumpet here, and blow a blast?"

"A trumpet blast or a yell. There's been a lot of yelling lately. At Queen Califia's, or here, for King Tut."

"And then there's the priest. Rattigan," Crumley said. "Didn't Constance try to blow his church down? But hell, look, we're standing on Omaha Beach, Normandy, over

Churchill's war rooms, holding Chamberlain's damned umbrella. You soaking it up?"

"Wading three feet deep. I wonder how it felt, that last second when old Rattigan drowned in this flood. Franco's Falangists, Hitler's youth, Stalin's Reds, Detroit's riots, Mayor La Guardia reading the Sunday funnies, what a death!"

"To hell with it. Look."

The remnant of Clarence Rattigan's burial cot was sticking up out of a cat litter of STOCK MARKET CRASHES and BANKS CLOSE. I picked up a final discard. Nijinsky danced on the theater page.

"A couple of nuts," said Crumley. "Nijinsky, and old Rattigan, who saved this review!"

"Touch your eyelids."

Crumley did so. His fingers came away wet.

"Damn," he said. "This is a graveyard. Move!"

I grabbed TOKYO SUES FOR PEACE . . .

And then headed for the sea.

Crumley drove me to my old beach apartment, but it was raining again, and I looked at the ocean threatening to drown us all with a storm that could knock at midnight and bring Constance, dead, and the other Rattigan, also dead, and crush my bed with rain and seaweed. Hell! I yanked Clarence Rattigan's newspapers off the wall.

Crumley drove me back to my small empty tract house, with no storm on the shore, and stashed vodka by my bed, Crumley's Elixir, and left the lights on and said he would call later that night to see if my soul was decent, and drove away.

I heard hail on the roof. Someone thumping a coffin lid.

I called Maggie across a continent of rain.

"Do I hear someone crying?" she said.

CHAPTER SEVENTEEN

THE sun was long gone when my phone rang.

"You know what time it is?" said Crumley.

"Ohmigod, it's night!"

"People dying takes a lot out of you. You done blubbering? I can't stand hysterical sob sisters, or bastard sons who carry Kleenex."

"Am I your bastard son?"

"Hit the shower, brush your teeth, and get the *Daily News* off your porch. I rang your bell, but you were lost. Did Queen Califia tell your fortune? She *should* have told her own."

"Is she—?"

"I'm heading back to Bunker Hill at seven-thirty. Be out front with a clean shirt and an umbrella!"

I was out front with a clean shirt and an umbrella at seven

twenty-nine. When I got in, Crumley grabbed my chin and scanned my face.

"Hey, no stormy weather!"

And we roared to Bunker Hill.

Passing Callahan and Ortega seemed different suddenly. There were no police cars or morgue wagons.

"You know a scotch ale called Old Peculiar?" said Crumley as we pulled up to the curb. "Look at the nonevent outside Queen Califia's."

I also looked at the newspaper in my lap. Califia wasn't a headliner. She was buried near the obits.

" 'Renowned psychic, famed in silent films, dies in fall. Alma Crown, a.k.a. Queen Califia, was found on the steps of her Bunker Hill residence. Neighbors reported hearing her peacock cry. Searching, Califia fell. Her book *The Chemistry of Palmistry* was a 1939 bestseller. Her ashes are to be strewn in the Egyptian Valley of the Kings, where, some said, she was born.' "

"Garbage," said Crumley.

We saw someone on the front porch of the Queen's house and walked up. It was a young woman in her twenties, with long dark hair and Gypsy coloring, wringing her hands, moaning, and letting tears fall, pointing her face toward the front door.

"Awful," she mourned. "Oh, awful, awful."

I opened the front door and stared in.

"No, my God, no."

Crumley came to look in at the desolation.

For the house was completely empty. All the pictures,

crystal balls, tarot cards, lamps, books, records, furniture
had vanished. Some mysterious van and transfer company
had lugged it all away.

I walked into the small kitchen, pulled open drawers.
Empty, vacuumed clean. Pantry: no spices, canned fruit.
The cupboard was bare, so her poor dog had none.

In her bedroom the closet was crammed with hangers but
no tent-size dressing gowns, stockings, shoes.

Crumley and I went out to stare at the young Gypsy
woman's face. "I saw it all!" she cried, pointing in all directions. "They stole everything! They're all poor. Excuses!
Poor! Across the street, when the police left, they knocked
me down, old women, men, kids, yelling, laughing, ran in
and out, carrying chairs, drapes, pictures, books. Grab this,
grab that! A fiesta! One hour and it was empty. They went
to that house over there! My God, the laughs. Look, my
hands, the blood! You want Califia's junk? Go knock on
doors! You gonna go?"

Crumley and I sat down on either side of her. Crumley
took her left hand. I took her right.

"Sonsabitches," she gasped. "Sonsabitches."

"That's about it," said Crumley. "You can go home.
There's nothing to guard. Nothing inside."

"*She* is inside. They took her body, but she's still there. I'll
wait until she says go."

We both looked over her shoulder at the screen door and
some unseen massive ghost.

"How will you know when she says go?"

The Gypsy wiped her eyes. "I'll know."

"Where are *you* going?" said Crumley.

Because I was on the walk heading across the street. At the opposite house I knocked.

Silence. I knocked again.

I peered through a side window. I could see shapes of furniture in midfloor, where there should be no furniture, and too many lamps, and rolled carpets.

I kicked the door and cursed and went to the middle of the street and was about to yell at every door when the Gypsy girl came quietly to touch my arm.

"I can go now," she said.

"Califia?"

"Said okay."

"Where to?" Crumley nodded at his car.

She could not stop staring at Califia's home, the center of all California.

"I have friends near the Red Rooster Plaza. Could you—"

"I could," said Crumley.

The Gypsy looked back at the vanishing palace of a queen.

"I will be back tomorrow," she called.

"She *knows* you will," I said.

We passed Callahan and Ortega, but this time Crumley ignored it.

We were quiet on the way to the plaza named for a rooster of a certain color.

We dropped the Gypsy.

"My God," I said on the way back, "it's like a friend, years ago, died, and the immigrants from Cuernavaca poured in, grabbed his collection of old 1900 phonographs, Caruso records, Mexican masks. Left his place like the Egyptian tombs, empty."

"That's what it's like to be poor," said Crumley.

"I grew up poor. I never stole."

"Maybe you never had a real chance."

We passed Queen Califia's place a final time.

"She's in there, all right. The Gypsy was right."

"She was right. But you're nuts."

"All this," I said. "It's too much. Too much. Constance hands me two wrong-number phone books and flees. We almost drown in twenty thousand leagues of old newspapers. Now, a dead queen. Makes me wonder, is Father Rattigan okay?"

Crumley swerved the car to the curb near a phone booth. "Here's a dime!"

In the phone booth I dialed the cathedral.

"Is Mister . . ." I blushed. "*Father* Rattigan . . . is he all right?"

"*All right?* He's at confession!"

"Good," I said foolishly, "as long as the one he's *confessing* is okay."

"Nobody," said the voice, "is *ever* okay!"

I heard a click. I dragged myself back to the car. Crumley eyed me like a dog's dinner. "Well?"

"He's alive. Where are we going?"

"Who knows. From here on, this trip is a retreat. You know Catholic retreats? Long silent weekends. Shut la trap. Okay?"

We drove to Venice City Hall. Crumley got out and slammed his door.

He was gone half an hour. When he returned he stuck his head in the driver's-side window and said, "Now hear this, I just took a week's sick leave. And, Jesus, this *is* sick. We got one week to find Constance, shield St. Vibiana's priest, raise the Lazarus dead, and warn your wife to stop me from strangling you. Nod your head yes."

I nodded.

"Next twenty-four hours you don't speak without permission! Now where are those goddamn phone books?"

I handed him the Books of the Dead.

Crumley, behind the wheel, scowled at them.

"Say one last thing and shut up!"

"You're still my pal!" I blurted.

"Pity," he said, and banged the gas.

CHAPTER EIGHTEEN

WE went back to Rattigan's and stood down on the shoreline. It was early evening and her lights were still full on; the place was like a full moon and a rising sun of architecture. Gershwin was still manhandling Manhattan one moment, Paris the next.

"I bet they buried him in his piano," said Crumley.

We got out the one Book of the Dead, Rattigan's personal phone pals, mostly cold and buried, and repeated what we had done before. Went through it page by page, with a growing sense of mortality.

On page 30 we came to the *R*s.

There it was: Clarence Rattigan's dead phone and a red Christian cross over his name.

"Damn. Now let's check Califia again."

We riffled back and there it was, with big red lines under her name and a crucifix.

"That means—?"

"Whoever planted this book with Constance marked all the names with red ink and a cross, handed it over, and then killed the first two victims. Maybe. I'm running half-empty."

"Or, hoping Constance would see the red ink crucifixes, *before* they were killed, panic on that night she came running, and destroy them inadvertently with her shouts. Christ! Let's check the other red lines and crosses. Check St. Vibiana's."

Crumley turned the pages and exhaled. "Red crucifix."

"But Father Rattigan's still *alive!*" I said. "Hell!"

I trudged up the sand to Rattigan's poolside phone. I dialed St. Vibiana's.

"Who's this?" a sharp voice answered.

"Father Rattigan! Thank God!"

"For what?"

"This is Constance's friend. The idiot."

"Dammit!" the priest cried.

"Don't take any more confessions tonight!"

"You giving orders?"

"Father, you're *alive!* I mean, well, is there anything we can do to protect you, or—"

"No, no!" the voice cried. "Go to that other heathen church! That *Jack and the Beanstalk* place!"

The telephone slammed.

I looked at Crumley, he looked at me.

"Look under Grauman's," I said.

Crumley looked. "Chinese, yeah. And Grauman's name. And a red circle and a crucifix. But he died *years* ago!"

"Yeah, but part of Constance is buried there, or written there in cement. I'll show you. Last chance to see *Jack and the Beanstalk?*"

"If we time it," said Crumley, "the film will be over."

CHAPTER NINETEEN

WE didn't have to time it right.

When Crumley dropped me in front of the Other Church, the great loud boisterous romantic tearstained celluloid cathedral . . . There was a sign on the red Chinese front door, CLOSED FOR ALTERATIONS, and some workmen moving in and out. A few people were in the forecourt, fitting their shoes in the footprints.

Crumley dropped me and vamoosed.

I turned to look at the great pagoda facade. Ten percent Chinese, ninety percent Grauman's. Little Sid's.

He was, some said, knee-high to a midget, the eighth Dwarf Cinema Munchkin, all four feet bursting with film clips, sound tracks, Kong shrieking on the Empire State Colman in Shangri-la, friend to Garbo, Dietrich, and H̶. burn, haberdasher to Chaplin, golf buddy to Laurel and

Hardy, keeper of the flame, recollector of ten thousand Pasts . . . Sid, pourer of cement, imprinter of fair and flat feet, begging and getting pavement autographs.

And there I stood on a lava flow of signatures of ghosts who had abandoned their shoe sizes.

I watched the tourists quietly testing their feet in the vast spread of cement prints, laughing softly.

What a church, I thought. More worshipers here than at St. Vibiana's.

"Rattigan," I whispered. "Are you *here?*"

CHAPTER TWENTY

IT was said that Constance Rattigan had the smallest tootsies in all Hollywood, perhaps in the whole world. She had
her shoes cobbled in Rome, and airmailed to her twice a
year because her old ones were melted from champagne
poured by crazed suitors. Small feet, dainty toes, tiny shoes.

Her imprints left in Grauman's cement the night of Au-
gust 22, 1929, proved this. Girls testing their size found
their feet to be titanic and pitiful and abandoned her prints
in despair.

So here I was alone on a strange night in Grauman's forecourt, the only place in dead, unburied Hollywood where
shoppers brought dreams for refunds.

The crowd cleared. I saw her footprints some twenty feet
away. I froze.

Because a small man in a black trench coat, a snap-brim

hat yanked over his brow, had just tucked his shoes in Rattigan's footprints.

"Jesus God," I gasped. "They *fit!*"

The small man gazed at his tiny shoes. For the first time in forty years, Rattigan's tracks were occupied.

"Constance," I whispered.

The small man's shoulders shrank.

"Right behind you," I whispered.

"Are you one of them?" I heard a voice say from under the large dark hat.

"One of what?" I said.

"Are you Death chasing me?"

"Just a friend trying to keep up."

"I've been waiting for you," the voice said, not moving, the feet planted firmly in the footprints of Constance Rattigan.

"What's it mean?" I said. "Why this wild goose chase? Are you scared or playing tricks?"

"Why would you say that?" the voice said, hidden.

"Good grief," I said. "Is this all some cheap dodge? Someone said you might want to write your life and needed someone to help. If you expect that to be me, no thanks. I've got better things to do."

"What's better than *me?*" said the voice, growing smaller.

"No one, but is Death really after you or are you looking for a new life, God knows what kind?"

"What better than Uncle Sid's concrete mortuary? All the names with nothing beneath. Ask away."

"Are you going to turn and face me?"

"I couldn't talk then."

"Is this some way of getting me to help you uncover your past? Is the casket half-full or half-empty? Did someone else make those red marks in your Book of the Dead, or did you make them?"

"It had to be someone else. Or else why would I be so frightened? Those red ink marks? I've got to look them up, find which ones are dead already, and which are just about to die but still alive. Do you ever have the feeling everything's falling apart?"

"Not *you*, Constance."

"Christ, yes! Some nights I sleep Clara Bow, wake up Noah, wet with vodka. Is my face ruined?"

"A lovely ruin."

"But still—"

Rattigan stared out at Hollywood Boulevard. "Once there were *real* tourists. Now it's torn shirts. Everything's lost, junior. Venice pier drowned, trolley tracks sunk. Hollywood and Vine, was it ever there?"

"Once. When the Brown Derby hung their walls with cartoons of Gable and Dietrich, and the headwaiters were Russian princes. Robert Taylor and Barbara Stanwyck drove by in their roadster. Hollywood and Vine? You planted your feet there and knew pure joy."

"You talk nice. Want to know where Mama's been?"

She moved her arm. She took some newspaper clippings from beneath her coat. I saw the names Califia and Mount Lowe.

"I was there, Constance," I said. "The old man was crushed by a collapsed haystack of news. God, it looked like he died on the San Andreas fault. Someone pushed the stacks, I think. An indecent burial. And Queen Califia? A fall downstairs. And your brother, the priest. Did you visit all three, Constance?"

"I don't have to answer."

"Let me try a different question. Do you like yourself?"

"What!?"

"Look. I like myself. I'm not perfect, hell no, but I never bedded anyone if I felt they were breakable. Lots of men say hit the hay, live! Not me. Even when it's offered on a plate. So with no sins, I don't often have bad dreams. Oh, sure, there was the time I ran away from my grandma when I was a kid, ran away and left her blocks behind, so she came home weeping. I still can't forgive myself. Or hitting my dog, just once, I hit him. And that still hurts, thirty years later. Not much of a list, right, to make bad dreams?"

Constance stood very still.

"God, God," she said, "how I wish I had your dreams."

"Ask and I'll give you the loan."

"You poor dumb innocent stupid kid. That's why I love you. Somewhere, at heaven's gate, can I trade in my old chimney soot nightmares for fresh clean angel wings?"

"Ask your brother."

"He threw me downstairs to hell long ago."

"You haven't answered my question. Do you like yourself?"

"What I see in the mirror, sure. It's what's inside the glass, deep under, scares me. I wake late nights with all that stuff swimming behind my face. Christ, that's sad. Can you help me?"

"How? I don't know which is which, you or your mirror. What's up front, what's beneath."

Constance shifted her feet.

"Can't you stand still?" I said. "If I say 'red light,' stop. Your feet are stuck in that cement. What then?"

I saw her shoes ache to pull free.

"People are staring at us!"

"The theater's closed. Most of the lights are out. The forecourt is empty."

"You don't understand. I've got to go. Straight on."

I looked up at the front doors of Grauman's, still open, with some workmen carrying equipment inside.

"It's the next step, but God, how do I get there?"

"Just walk."

"You don't understand. It's hopscotch. There must be other footprint paths to the door, if I can find them. Which way do I jump?"

Her head moved. The dark hat fell to the pavement. Constance's close-cropped bronze hair came into view. She still stared ahead, as if afraid to show me her face.

"If I say go, what then?" I asked.

"I'll go."

"And meet me again, where?"

"God knows. Quick! Say 'go.' They're catching up."

"Who?"

"All those others. They'll kill me if I don't kill first. You wouldn't want me to die right here? Well, would you?"

I shook my head.

"Ready, set, go?" she asked.

"Ready, set."

And she was gone.

She zigzagged across the forecourt, a dozen fast steps to the right, another dozen to the left, pause, and a final two dozen steps to a third set of prints, where she froze, as if it were a land mine.

A car horn hooted. I turned. When I glanced back, the Grauman's front door swallowed a shadow.

I counted to ten to give her a real start, then I bent down to pick up the tiny shoes she had left behind in her footprints. Then I walked over to the first set of prints where she had paused. Sally Simpson, 1926. The name was just an echo from a lost time.

I moved on to the second set of prints. Gertrude Erhard, 1924. An even fainter ghost of time. And the final footprints nearer the front door. Dolly Dawn, 1923. *Peter Pan.*

Dolly Dawn? A fleeting mist of years touched me. I almost remembered.

"Hell," I whispered. "No way."

And got ready to let Uncle Sid's fake Chinese palace swallow me with one huge dark dragon swallow.

CHAPTER TWENTY-ONE

I STOPPED just outside the crimson doors, for as clearly as if he were calling, I heard Father Rattigan shout, "Lamentable!"

Which made me pull out Rattigan's Book of the Dead.

I had only looked for names, now I looked for a place. There it was under the *G*s: Grauman's. Followed by an address and a name: Clyde Rustler.

Rustler, I thought, my God, he retired from acting in 1920 after working with Griffith and Gish and getting involved with Dolly Dimples's bathtub death. And here was his name—alive?—on a boulevard where they buried you without warning and erased you from history the way dear Uncle Joe Stalin rubbed out his pals, with a shotgun eraser.

And, my heart thumped, there was red ink around his name and a double crucifix.

Rattigan—I looked at the dark beyond the red door—

Rattigan, yes, but Clyde Rustler, are you here, too? I reached and grasped one brass handle and a voice behind me announced bleakly: "There's nothing inside to steal!"

A gaunt homeless guy stood to my right, dressed in various shades of gray, speaking to the universe. He felt my gaze.

"Go ahead." I read his lips. "You got nothing to lose."

Plenty to win, I thought, but how do you excavate a big Chinese tomb filled with black-and-white flicker film clips, an aviary of birds shuttling the air, fireworks ricocheting a big ravenous screen, as swift as memory, as quick as remorse?

The homeless man waited for me to self-destruct with remembrance. I nodded. I smiled.

And as quickly as Rattigan, I sank into the theater's darkness.

CHAPTER TWENTY-TWO

INSIDE the lobby there was a frozen army of Chinese coolies, concubines, and emperors, dressed in ancient wax, parading nowhere.

One of the wax figurines blinked. "Yes?"

God, I thought, a crazy outside, a crazy in, and Clyde Rustler moldering toward ninety or ninety-five.

Time shifted. If I ducked back out, I would find a dozen drive-ins where teenage waitresses roller-skated hamburgers.

"Yes?" the Chinese wax mannequin said again.

I moved swiftly through the first entry door and down the aisle under the balcony, where I stared up.

It was a big dark aquarium, undersea. It was possible to imagine a thousand film ghosts, scared by gunshot whispers, soaring to flake the ceiling and vanish in the vents. Melville's whale sailed there, unseen, *Old Ironsides,* the *Titanic.* The

Bounty, sailing forever, never reaching port. I focused my gaze on up through the multiple balconies toward what had once been called nigger heaven.

My God, I thought, I'm three years old.

That was the year when Chinese fairy tales haunted my bed, whispered by a favorite aunt, when I thought death was just a forever bird, a silent dog in the yard. My grandfather was yet to lie in a box at a funeral parlor, while Tut arose from his tomb. What, I asked, was Tut famous for? For being dead four thousand years. Boy, I said, how'd he *do* that?

And here I was in a vast tomb under the pyramid, where I had always wished to be. If you lifted the aisle carpets, you'd find the lost pharaohs buried with fresh loaves of bread and bright sprigs of onions; food for far-traveling up-river to Eternity.

They must never ruin this, I thought. I must be buried here.

"It's not Green Glade Cemetery," said the old wax Chinaman nearby, reading my mind.

I had spoken aloud.

"When was this theater built?" I murmured.

The old waxwork let loose a forty-day flood: "1921, one of the first. There was nothing here, some palm trees, farm-houses, cottages, a dirt main street, little bungalows built to lure Doug Fairbanks, Lillian Gish, Mary Pickford. Radio was just a crystal matchbox with earphones. Nobody could hear the future on that. We opened big. People walked or drove from Melrose north. Saturday nights there were veritable desert caravans of movie fanatics. The graveyard hadn't yet begun at Gower and Santa Monica. It filled up with Valentino's ruptured appendix in '26. At Grauman's opening night, Louis B. Mayer arrived from the Selig Zoo in Lincoln Park. That's where MGM got their lion. Mean, but no teeth. Thirty dancing girls. Will Rogers spun rope. Trixie Friganza sang her famous 'I Don't Care' and wound up an extra in a Swanson film, 1934. Go down, stick your nose in the old basement dressing rooms, you'll find leftover underwear from those flappers who died for love of Lowell Sherman. Dapper guy with mustache, cancer got him, '34. You listening?"

"Clyde Rustler," I blurted.

"Holy Jesus! Nobody knows *him!* See way up, that old projection room? They buried him there alive in '29 when they built the new projection room on the second balcony."

I stared up into phantoms of mist, rain and Shangri-la snow seeking the High Lama.

My shadow friend said: "No elevator. Two hundred steps!"

A long climb, with no Sherpas, up to a middle lobby and a mezzanine and then another balcony and another after that amid three thousand seats. How do you please three thousand customers? I wondered. How? If eight-year-old boys didn't pee three times during your film, you had it made!

I climbed.

I stopped halfway to sit, panting, suddenly ancient instead of halfway new.

CHAPTER TWENTY-THREE

I REACHED the back wall of Mount Everest and tapped on the old projection-room door.

"Is that who I think it is?" a terrified voice cried.

"No," I said quietly, "just me. Back for one last matinée after forty years."

That was a stroke of genius; upchucking my past.

The terrified voice simmered down.

"What's the password?"

It came right off my tongue, a boy's voice.

"Tom Mix and his horse, Tony. Hoot Gibson. Ken Maynard. Bob Steele. Helen Twelvetrees. Vilma Banky . . ."

"That'll do."

It was a long while before I heard a giant spider brush the door panel. The door whined. A silver shadow leaned out, a living metaphor of the black-and-white phantoms I had seen flickering across the screen a lifetime ago.

"No one ever comes up here," said this old, old man.

"*No* one?"

"No one ever *knocks* on my door," said the man with silver hair and silver face and silver clothes, bleached out by seventy years of living under a rock in a high place and gazing down at unreality ten thousand times. "No one knows I'm here. Not even me."

"You're here. You're Clyde Rustler."

"Am I?" For a moment I thought he might body-search his suspenders and sleeve garters.

"Who are you?" He poked his face like a turtle's from its shell.

I said my name.

"Never heard of you." He glanced down at the empty screen. "You one of *them?*"

"The dead stars?"

"They sometimes climb up. Fairbanks came last night."

"Zorro, D'Artagnan, Robin Hood? *He* knocked at your door?"

"*Scratched.* Being dead has its problems. You coming in or out?"

I stepped in quickly before he could change his mind.

The film projectors stood facing emptiness in a room that looked like a Chung King burial chamber. It smelled of dust and sand and acrid celluloid. There was only one chair between the projectors. As he'd said, no one ever came to visit.

I stared at the crowded walls. There must've been three

dozen pictures nailed there, some in cheap Woolworth frames, others in silver, still others mere scraps torn from old *Silver Screen* magazines, photographs of thirty women, no two alike.

The old, old man let a smile haunt his face.

"My sweetheart dears, from when I was an active volcano."

The most ancient of ancient men looked out at me from behind a maze of wrinkles, the kind you get when you search the icebox at six A.M. and take out last night's premixed martinis.

"I keep the door locked. I thought you were just here, yelling outside."

"Not me."

"Someone was. Outside of that, nobody's been up here since Lowell Sherman died."

"That's two obituaries in ten minutes. Winter 1934. Cancer and pneumonia."

"*Nobody* knows that!"

"I roller-skated by the Coliseum one Saturday 1934 before a football game. Lowell Sherman came in whooping and barking. I got his autograph and said, 'Take care.' He died two days later."

"Lowell Sherman." The old, old man regarded me with a new luster in his eyes. "As long as *you're* alive, he is, too."

Clyde Rustler collapsed in the one chair and sized me up again. "Lowell Sherman. Why in hell did you make the long climb up here? People have died climbing. Uncle Sid climbed up once or twice, said to hell with it, built the bigger projection booth a thousand yards downslope in the real world, if there is a real one. Never went down to see. So?"

For he saw that I was casting my gaze around his primeval nest at those walls teeming with dozens of faces, forever young.

"Would you like a rundown on these mountain-lion street cats?" He leaned and pointed.

"Her name was Carlotta or Midge or Diana. She was a Spanish flirt, a Cal Coolidge 'It girl' with a skirt up to her navel, a Roman queen fresh out of DeMille's milk bath. Then she was a vamp named Illysha, a typist called Pearl, an English tennis player—Pamela. Sylvia? Ran a nudist flytrap in Cheyenne. Some called her 'Hard Hearted Hannah the Vamp of Savannah.' Dressed like Dolley Madison, sang 'Tea for Two,' 'Chicago,' popped out of a big clamshell like the pearl of paradise, Flo Ziegfeld's craze. Fired by her father at thirteen for conduct unbecoming a human who ripened fast: Willa-Kate. Worked in a chophouse chink joint: Lila Wong. Got more votes than the president, Coney Island Beauty Pageant, '29: not-so-plain Willa. Got off the night train in Glendale: Barbara Jo, next day, almost, head of Glory Films: Anastasia Alice Grimes—"

He stopped. I looked up. "Which brings us to Rattigan," I said.

Clyde Rustler froze in place.

"You said no one's been up here for years. But—she came up here today, right? Maybe to look at these pictures? Did she or didn't she?"

The old, old man stared at his dusty hands, then slowly rose to face a brass whistle tube in the wall, one of those submarine devices that you blew so it shrieked and you yelled orders.

"Leo? Wine! A two-dollar tip!"

A tiny voice squealed from the brass nozzle, "You don't *drink!*"

"I do now, Leo. And hot dogs!"

The brass nozzle squealed and died.

The old, old man grunted and stared at the wall. A long, terribly long five minutes passed. While we waited I opened my notepad and took down the names scrawled on the pictures. Then we heard the hot dogs and wine rattling up the dumbwaiter. Clyde Rustler stared as if he had forgotten that tiny elevator. He took forever opening the wine with a corkscrew, sent by Leo, from down below. There was only one glass.

"One," he apologized. "You first. I'm not afraid of catching anything."

"I got nothing for you to catch." I drank and handed the glass over. He drank and I could see the relaxation move his body.

"And now?" he said. "Let me show you some clips I glued together. Why? Last week a stranger called from down below. That voice on the phone. Was once Harry Cohn's live-in nurse, never said yes, but yes, yes, Harry, yes! Said she was looking for Robin Locksley. *Robin Hood.* Searching for Robin of Locksley. An actress took that name, a flash in the pan. She disappeared in Hearst's castle or his backside kitchen. But now this voice, years later, asks for Locksley. Spooked me. I ran through my cans and found the one film she made in 1929, when sound really took over. Watch."

He fitted the film into the projector and switched on the lamp. The image shot down to flood the big screen.

On the screen a circus butterfly spun, flirting her gossamer wings, dropping, to pull the bit from her smile, laugh, then run, pursued by white knights and black villains. "Recognize her?"

"Nope."

"Try *this*." He spun the film. The screen filled with a smoldering bank of snow fires, a Russian noblewoman, smoking long languid cigarettes, wringing her handkerchief, someone had died or was going to die.

"Well?" said Clyde Rustler hopefully.

"Nope."

"Try again!"

The projector lit the darkness with 1923; a tomboy climbing a tree to shake down fruit, laughing, but you could see small crab apples under her shirtfront.

"*Tomboy Sawyer*. A girl! Who? Damn!"

The old man filled the screen with a dozen more images, starting with 1925, ending with 1952, open, shut, mysterious, obvious, light, dark, wild, composed, beautiful, plain, willful, innocent.

"You don't know *any* of those? My God, I've racked my brain. There must be some reason why I've saved these damned clips. Look at me, dammit! Know how old I am?"

"Around ninety, ninety-five?"

"Ten thousand years! Jesus. They found me floating in a basket on the Nile! I fell downhill with the Tablets. I doused the fire in the burning bush. Mark Antony said, 'Loose the dogs of war'; I loosed the lot. Did I know all these wonders? I wake nights hitting my head to make the jelly beans shake in place. Every time I've almost got the answer, I move my head and the damned beans fall. You sure you don't remember these clips or the faces on the wall? Good grief, we've got a mystery!"

"I was about to say the same. I came up here because someone else came. Maybe that voice that called from down below."

"What voice?"

"Constance Rattigan," I said.

I let the fog settle behind his eyes.

"What's she got to do with this?" he wondered.

"Maybe *she* knows. Last time I saw her she was standing in her own footprints."

"And you think she might know who all these faces belong to, what all the names mean? Hold on. Outside the door . . . I guess it was today. Can't be yesterday. Today she said, 'Hand 'em over!'"

"Hand what over?"

"Hell, what do you see in this damn empty place worth handing over?"

I looked at the pictures on the wall. Clyde Rustler saw my look.

"Why would anyone want those?" he said. "Not worth nothing. Even I don't know why in hell I nailed them there. Are they wives or some old girlfriends?"

"How many of each did you have?"

"I don't have the fingers to count."

"One thing for sure, Constance wanted you to hand 'em over. Was she jealous?"

"Constance? You got road rage in the streets, she had bed rage. Wanted to grab all my lovelies, whoever in hell they were, and stomp, tear, and burn them. Go on. Finish the wine. I got things to do."

"Like what?"

But he was rethreading the film clips in the projector, fascinated by a thousand and one nights past.

I moved along the wall and scribbled furiously, writing down the names under all of the pictures, and then said:

"If Constance comes back, will you let me know?"

"For the pictures? I'll throw her downstairs."

"Someone else said that. Only it was to hell instead of the second balcony. Why would you throw her?"

"There's gotta be a reason, right? Don't recollect! And why did you say you climbed up here? And what was it you called me?"

"Clyde Rustler."

"Oh, yeah. Him. It just came to me. Did you know I am Constance's father?"

"What!?"

"Constance's father. I thought I told you before. Now you can leave. Good night."

I went out and shut the door on whoever that was and the pictures on the wall, whoever they were.

CHAPTER TWENTY-FOUR

DOWNSTAIRS, I edged to the front of the theater and stared down. Then I stepped into the orchestra pit, and edged to the back wall and peered though a door into a long hall that diminished into complete night and a night inside that night, where all the old abandoned dressing rooms were.

I was tempted to call a name.

But what if she answered?

Far off down that black corridor, I thought I heard the sound of a hidden sea, or a river flowing somewhere in the dark.

I put one foot forward and pulled back.

I heard that dark ocean heave on an endless shore again.

Then I turned, and went away up through the great darkness, out of the pit into the aisles with everyone gone, rushing toward the doors leading out to an evening sky most dearly welcome.

I carried Rattigan's incredibly small shoes over to her footprints and placed them neatly down to fit.

At which instant I felt my guardian angel touching my shoulder.

"You're back from the dead," said Crumley.

"You can say that again," I said, staring at the wide red doorway of Grauman's Chinese with all those film creatures swimming in the dark.

"She's in there," I murmured. "I wish I knew a way to get her out."

"Dynamite tied to a bundle of cash might do it."

"Crumley!"

"Sorry, I forgot we were talking about Florence Nightingale."

I stepped back. Crumley regarded Rattigan's tiny shoes lodged in prints put down a long, long time ago.

"Not exactly ruby slippers," he said.

CHAPTER TWENTY-FIVE

WE rode across town in a warm silence. I tried to describe the great black sea of Grauman's.

"There's this big dressing-room cellar, maybe full of stuff from 1925, 1930. I have a feeling she might be *there*."

"Save your breath," said Crumley.

"Someone's got to go down there to see."

"You afraid to go there alone?"

"Not exactly."

"That means damn right! Shut up and ride shotgun."

We were soon at Crumley's. He put a cold beer against my brow.

"Hold it there until you feel it cure your thinking."

I held it there. Crumley switched on the TV and began switching through the channels.

"I don't know which is worse," he said, "your gab or the local TV news."

"Father Seamus Rattigan," the TV said.

"Hold it!" I cried.

Crumley switched back.

". . . Vibiana's Cathedral."

And a blizzard of static and snow.

Crumley hit the damned TV with his fist.

". . . Natural causes. Rumored to be future cardinal . . ."

Another snowstorm. And the TV went dead.

"I been meaning to have it fixed," said Crumley.

We both stared at his telephone, telling it to ring.

We both jumped.

Because it *did!*

CHAPTER TWENTY-SIX

IT was a woman, Father Rattigan's assistant, Betty Kelly, inarticulate, going down for the third time, begging for mercy.

I offered what small mercy I had, to come visit.

"Don't wait, or I'm dead myself," she wailed.

Betty Kelly was out in front of St. Vibiana's when Crumley and I arrived. We stood for a long moment before she saw us, gave a quick, half-realized wave, and dropped her gaze. We came to stand by her. I introduced Crumley.

"I'm sorry," I said.

She raised her head.

"Then you *are* the one was talking to Father!" she said. "Oh, Lord, let's get inside."

The big doors were locked for the night. We went in

through a door at the side. Inside she swayed and almost fell. I caught and led her to one of the pews, where she sat breathless.

"We came as quick as we could," I said.

"You *knew* him?" She gasped. "It's so confusing. You knew someone in common, an acquaintance, a friend?"

"A relative," said Crumley. "The same name."

"Rattigan! She killed him. Wait!" She grabbed my sleeve. For I was on my feet.

"Sit," she gasped. "I don't mean murder. But she killed him."

I sat back down, gone cold. Crumley backed off. She clutched my elbow and lowered her voice.

"She was here, sometimes three times a day, in confession, whispering, then raving. Poor Father looked like he'd been shot when she left, but she hardly left, just stayed until he fell out starving, couldn't eat, and the liquor cabinet low. He let her rave. Later I'd check the confessional: empty. But the air smelled like it had been hit by lightning. She kept shouting the *same* thing."

"What?"

"'I'm killing them, killing them!' she yelled. 'And I'll keep on killing them until I've killed them all. Help me to kill them, bless their souls! Then I'll kill the rest. Kill them all! Get them off my back, out of my life! Then, Father,' she cried, 'I'll be free, clean! But help me bury them so they won't come back! Help me!'

"'Off! Away!' Father yelled. 'My God, what are you asking me to do?'

"'Help me put them away, pray over them so they won't come back, stay dead! Say yes!'

"'Get out!' Father cried, and then she said worse."

"What?"

"She said, 'Then damn you, damn, damn, damn you to hell!' Her voice was so loud, people left. I could hear her weeping. The Father must have been in a state of shock. Then I heard footsteps running in the dark. I waited for Father Rattigan to speak, say anything. Then I dared open the door. He was there. And silent because . . . he was dead."

And here the secretary let the tears shed themselves down her cheeks.

"Poor man," she said. "Those dreadful words stopped his heart, as they almost stopped mine. We must find that awful woman. Make her take back the words so he can live again. God, what am I saying? Him slumped there as if she had drained his blood. You know her? Tell her she's done her worst. There, I've said it. Now I've thrown up, and where do *you* go to be clean? It's yours, and sorry I did it to you."

I looked down at my suit as if expecting to find her vile upchuck.

Crumley walked over to the confessional and opened both doors and stared in at the darkness. I came to stand next to him and take a deep breath.

"Smell it?" said Betty Kelly. "It's there and ruined. I've told the cardinal to tear it down and burn it."

I took a final breath. A touch of charcoal and St. Elmo's fires.

Crumley closed the doors.

"It won't help," Betty Kelly said. "She's still there. So is he, poor soul, dead tired and dead. Two coffins, side by side. God help us. I've used you all up. You have the same look the poor father had."

"Don't tell me that," I said weakly.

"I won't," she said.

And led by Crumley, I beggared my way to the door.

CHAPTER TWENTY-SEVEN

I COULDN'T nap, I couldn't stay awake, I couldn't write, I couldn't think. At last, confused and maddened, very late I called St. Vibiana's again.

When at last Betty Kelly answered she sounded like she was in a cave of torments.

"I can't talk!"

"Quickly!" I begged. "You remember all she said in the confessional? Anything else important, consequential, different?"

"Dear God," said Betty Kelly. "Words and words and words. But wait. She kept saying you must forgive *all* of us! All of us, every one! There was no one in the booth but her. *All* of us, she said. You still there?"

At last I said, "I'm here."

"Is there more you want?"

"Not now."

I hung up.

"All of us," I whispered. "Forgive *all* of us!"

I called Crumley.

"Don't say it." He guessed. "No sleep tonight? And you want me to meet you at Rattigan's in an hour. You going to search the place?"

"Just a friendly rummage."

"Rummage! What is it, theory or hunch?"

"Pure reason."

"Sell that in a sack for night soil!"

Crumley was gone.

"He hang up on you?" I asked my mirror.

"Hung up on you," my mirror said.

CHAPTER TWENTY-EIGHT

THE phone rang. I picked it up as if it were red-hot.

"Is that the Martian?" a voice said.

"Henry!" I cried.

"That's me," the voice said. "It's crazy, but I miss you, son. Kinda dumb, a colored saying that to an ethnic flying-saucer pilot."

"I've never heard better," I said, choking up.

"Hell," said Henry, "if you start crying, I'm gone."

"Don't," I sniffled. "Oh God, Henry, how fine it is to hear your voice!"

"Which means you've milked the cow and got a bucket of I-won't-say. You want me polite or impolite?"

"Both, Henry. Things are nuts. Maggie's back east. I got Crumley here, of course, but—"

"Which means you need a blind man to find your way

out of a cowshed full of cowsheds, right? Hell, let me get my hankie." He blew his nose. "How soon do you need this all-seeing nose?"

"Yesterday."

"I'm there now! Hollywood, visiting some poor black trash."

"You know Grauman's Chinese?"

"Hell, yes!"

"How quickly can you meet me there?"

"As quick as you want, son. I'll be standing in Bill Robinson's tap-dancer shoes. Do we visit another graveyard?"

"Almost."

I called Crumley to say where I was going, that I might be late getting to Rattigan's, but that I'd be bringing Henry with me.

"The blind leading the blind," he said.

CHAPTER TWENTY-NINE

HE was standing exactly where he said he would be: in Bill Robinson's "copasetic" dancing footprints, not banished to that long-gone nigger heaven but out front where thousands of passing whites could see.

His body was erect and quiet, but his shoes were itching around in Bill Robinson's marks, ever so serenely. His eyes were shut, like his mouth, turned in on a pleased imagination.

I stood in front of him and exhaled.

Henry's mouth burst.

"Wrigley's Double Your Pleasure, Double Your Fun, with Wrigley's Doublemint, Doublemint Gum! Don't get it on me!" He laughed, seized my elbows. "Lord, boy, you look *fine!* I don't have to *see* to *know.* You've always sounded like some of those people up on the screen!"

"That comes from sneaking into too many movies."

"Let me feel you, boy. Hey, you been drinking lotsa malts!"

"You look swell, Henry."

"I always *wondered* what *I* looked like."

"The way Bill Robinson sounds is how you shape, Henry."

"Am I in his shoes here? Say yes."

"A perfect fit. Thanks for coming, Henry."

"Had to. It's one helluva time since we ransacked grave-yards! I go to sleep nights running those graves ahead or behind. What kind of graveyard's *here?*"

I glanced at Grauman's Oriental facade.

"Ghosts. That's what I said when I snuck backstage when I was six and stared up at all those black-and-white things leering on the screen. The Phantom playing the organ has his mask yanked off and jumps thirty feet tall to kill you with one stare. Pictures tall and wide and pale and the actors mostly dead. Ghosts."

"Did your folks hear you talk like that?"

"With them? Mum's the word."

"That's a nice son. I smell incense. Got to be Grauman's. Real class. No chop-suey name."

"Here goes, Henry. Let me hold the door."

"Hey, it's dark in there. You bring a flashlight? Always feels good to wave a flashlight and look like we know what we're doing."

"Here's the flashlight, Henry."

"Ghosts, you said?"

"Séances four times a day for thirty years."

"Don't hold my elbow, makes me feel useless. If I fall, shoot me!"

And he was off, hardly ricocheting down the aisle toward the orchestra pit and the great spaces beyond and below.

"It getting darker?" he said. "Let me turn on the flashlight."

He switched it on.

"There." He smiled. "*That's* better!"

CHAPTER THIRTY

IN the dark unlit basement, there were rooms and rooms and rooms, all with mirrors lining their walls, the reflections reflecting and re-reflecting, emptiness facing emptiness, corridors of lifeless sea.

We went into the first, biggest one. Henry circled the flashlight like a lighthouse beam.

"Plenty of ghosts down here."

The light hit and sank in the ocean deeps.

"Not the same as the ghosts upstairs. Spookier. I always wondered about mirrors and that thing called reflection. Another *you*, right? Four or five feet off, sunk under *ice?*" Henry reached out to touch the glass. "Someone *under* there?"

"You, Henry, and me."

"Hot damn. I sure wish I could know that."

We moved on along the cold line of mirrors.

And there they were. More than ghosts. Graffiti on glass. I must have sucked in my breath, for Henry swung his flashlight to my face.

"You *see* something *I* don't?"

"My God, yes!"

I reached out to the first cold Window on Time.

My finger came away smudged with a faint trace of ancient lipstick.

"Well?" Henry bent as if to squint at my discovery. "What?"

"Margot Lawrence. R.I.P. October 1923."

"Someone stash her here under glass?"

"Not quite. And over about three feet, another mirror: Juanita Lopez. Summer '24."

"Don't ring no bell."

"Next mirror: Carla Moore. Christmas, 1925."

"Hey," said Henry. "Silent film but a sighted friend spoke her to me one matinee. Carla Moore! She was something!"

I guided the flashlight.

"Eleanor Twelvetrees. April '26," I read.

"Helen Twelvetrees was in *The Cat and the Canary.*"

"This might've been her sister, but so many names were fake, you never know. Lucille LeSueur became Joan Crawford. Lily Chauchoin was reborn as Claudette Colbert. Gladys Smith: Carole Lombard. Cary Grant was Archibald Leach."

"You could run a quiz show." Henry extended his fingers. "What's this?"

"Jennifer Long: '29."

"Didn't she die?"

"Disappeared, about the time Sister Aimee sank in the sea and arose, reborn, on the Hallelujah shore."

"How many more names?"

"As many as there are mirrors."

Henry tasted one finger. "Yum! It's been a long time but—lipstick. What color?"

"Tangee Orange. Summer Heat Coty. Lanvier Cherry."

"Why do you figure these ladies wrote their names and dates?"

"Because, Henry, it wasn't a lot of ladies. One woman signed the names, all different."

"One woman who wasn't a lady? Hold my cane while I think."

"You don't *have* a cane, Henry."

"Funny how your hand feels things not there. You want me to guess?"

I nodded even though Henry couldn't see; I knew he'd feel the rush of my bobbing head. I wanted him to say it, needed to hear him speak that name. Henry smiled at the mirrors, and his smile beamed one hundredfold.

"Constance."

His fingers touched the glass.

"The Rattigan," he said.

CHAPTER THIRTY-ONE

AGAIN, Henry leaned to brush a reddish signature and then touch it to his lips.

He moved to the next glass, repeated the gesture, and let his tongue figure.

"Different flavors," he noted.

"Like different women?"

"It all comes back." His eyes squeezed tight. "Lord, Lord. Lots of women passed through my hands, through my heart, came and went unseen; all those flavors. Why do I feel stopped up?"

"Because *I* feel the same way."

"Crumley says when you turn on the faucets, stand back. You're a good boy."

"I'm no boy."

"You sound like you're fourteen, when your voice changed and you tried to grow a mustache."

He moved and touched, then looked with his sightless eyes at the ancient residue on his fingers.

"All these have to do with Constance?"

"A hunch."

"You got a powerful stomach; I know from having your stuff read to me. My mama once said a powerful midsection is better than two brains. Most folks use their brains too much when they should be listening to that thing under their ribs. The gang—ganglion? My mama never called it that. House spider, she said. When she met some damn-fool politician, she always felt right above her stomach. If the spider was twitching, she'd smile: *yes*. But if the spider tightened into a ball, she shut her eyes: *no*. That's you.

"My mama read you. She said you don't write them weary stories (she meant *eerie*) with gray matter. You pull the spider legs under your ribs. My mama said, 'That boy will never be sick, never get poisoned by people, he knows how to upchuck, teasing that balled-up spider to let go.' She said, 'He don't stay up nights in a bad life, getting old while he's young. He'd make a great doctor, cut right to the pain and toss it out.'"

"Your mama said all that?" I blushed.

"Woman who got twelve kids, buried six, raised the rest. One bad husband, one good. She got fine ideas which side to use in bed so you untie, let your gut free."

"I wish I had met her."

"She's still around." Henry put his palm on his chest.

Henry surveyed the unseen mirrors, pulled his black glasses from his pocket, wiped and put them on.

"That's better. Rattigan, these names, was she crazy wild? Was she ever honest-to-God sane?"

"Offshore. I heard her swimming way out with the seals, barking, a free soul."

"Maybe she should have stayed out there."

"Herman Melville," I muttered.

"Say again?"

"Took me years to finish *Moby-Dick*. Melville should have stayed at sea with Jack, his loving friend. Land? When he lived there, it tore his soul from his heart. Onshore, he aged thirty years, in a customs shed, half-dead."

"Poor son of a bitch," whispered Henry.

"Poor son of a bitch," I echoed quietly.

"And Rattigan? You think she should've stayed offshore, not in her fancy beach place?"

"It was big, bright, white, and lovely, but a tomb full of ghosts, like those films upstairs forty feet tall, fifty years wide, like these mirrors here, and one woman hating them all for unknown reasons."

"Poor son of a bitch," murmured Henry.

"Poor bitch," I said.

CHAPTER THIRTY-TWO

"LET'S see some more," said Henry. "Switch on the lights so I won't need my cane."

"Can you feel if lights are on or off?"

"Silly child. Read me the names!"

I took his arm and we moved along the mirrors as I read the names.

"The dates under the names," Henry commanded. "They getting closer to *now?*"

1935. 1937. 1939. 1950. 1955.

And with names, names, names to go with them, all different.

"One too many," said Henry. "We done?"

"One last mirror and date. October thirty-first. Last year."

"How come everything happens to you on Halloween?"

"Fate and providence love wimps like me."

"You say the date, but . . ." Henry touched the cold glass. "No name?"

"None."

"She going to come *add* a name? Going to show up making noises just a dog hears, and no light down here. She—"

"Shut up, Henry." I stared along the mirrors in the cellar night where shadow-phantoms ran.

"Son." Henry took my arm. "Let's git."

"One last thing." I took a dozen steps and stopped.

"Don't tell me." Henry inhaled. "You're fresh out of floor."

I looked down at a round manhole. The darkness sank deep with no end.

"Sounds empty." Henry inhaled. "A freshwater *storm drain!*"

"Beneath the back of the theater, yes."

"Damn!"

For suddenly a flood of water gushed below, a clean tide smelling of green hills and cool air.

"It rained a few hours ago. Takes an hour for the runoff to get here. Most of the year the storm drain's dry. Now it'll run a foot deep, all the way to the ocean."

I bent to feel the inside of the hole. Rungs.

Henry guessed. "You're *not* climbing down?"

"It's dark and cold and a long way to the sea, and if you're careless, drowning."

Henry sniffed.

"You figure she came up this way to check those names?"

"Or came in through the theater and climbed down."

"Hey! *More* water!"

A gust of wind, very cold, sighed up out of the hole.

"Jesus Christ!" I yelled.

"What?"

I stared. "I *saw* something!"

"If you didn't, *I* did!" The flashlight beam arced crazily around the mirrored room as Henry grabbed my elbow and lurched away from the hole.

"We going the right way?"

"Christ," I said. "I *hope* so!"

CHAPTER THIRTY-THREE

OUR taxi dropped us at the curb behind Rattigan's big white Arabian fortress.

"Lordy," said Henry, and added, "That meter ran overtime. From now on, *I'm* driving."

Crumley was not out front by the shoreline but farther up by the pool with half a dozen full martini glasses, two already empty. He gazed at these fondly and explained.

"I'm ready now for your numbskull routines. I am *fortified.* Hello, Henry. Henry, aren't you sorry you left New Orleans for this can-o'-worms factory?"

"One of those drinks smells like vodka, right? *That* will make me not sorry."

I handed a glass to Henry and took one for myself in haste while Crumley scowled at my silence.

"Okay, spill it," he said.

I told him about Grauman's and the basement dressing-room mirrors. "Plus," I said, "I been making lists."

"Hold it. You've sobered me up," said Crumley. "Let me kill another." He lifted a glass in mock salute. "Okay, read your lists."

"The grocery boy on Mount Lowe. The neighbors of Queen Califia in Bunker Hill. Father Rattigan's secretary. The film projectionist on high in Grauman's Chinese."

Henry cut in. "That gent in Grauman's . . . ?"

I described Rustler, stashed among stacks of old film with the pictures on the walls of all the sad women with all the lost names.

Henry mused. "Hey now. Did you make a list of those ladies in the pictures up on high?"

I read off my pad: "Mabel. Helen. Marilee. Annabel. Hazel. Betty Lou. Clara. Pollyanna . . ."

Crumley sat up straight.

"You got a list of those names on the cellar mirrors?"

I shook my head. "It was *dark* down there."

"Easy as pie." Henry tapped his head. "Hazel. Annabel. Grace. Pollyanna. Helen. Marilee. Betty Lou. Detect the similarities?"

As the names rolled from Henry's mouth, I ticked them off my penciled list. A perfect match.

At which point there was a lightning strike. The lights failed. We could hear the surf roar in to salt Rattigan's beach as pale moonlight silvered the shore. Thunder clamored. It gave me time to think and say, "Rattigan's got a complete run of Academy annuals with all the pictures, ages, roles.

Her competition is in every one. It ties in with all those up-stairs pictures, downstairs mirrors, right?"

Thunder echoed, the lights blinked back on.

We went inside and got out the Academy books.

"Look for the mirror names," Henry advised.

"I know, I know," Crumley growled.

In half an hour we had thirty years of Academy annuals paper-clipped.

"Ethel, Carlotta, Suzanne, Clara, Helen," I read.

"Constance can't hate them all."

"Chances are," said Henry. "What else she got in her bookshelves?"

An hour later we found some actors' reference albums, crammed with pictures, going way back. One with a legend up front giving the name J. Wallington Bradford. I read, "A.k.a. Tallullah Two, a.k.a. Swanson, Gloria in Excelsius, a.k.a. Funny Face."

A quiet bell sounded in the back of my head.

I opened another album and read: "Alberto Quickly. Fast flimflammery. Plays all parts *Great Expectations*. Acts *A Christmas Carol, Christmas Carol's* Scrooge, Marley, Three Christmases, Fezziwig. *Saint Joan*, unburned. Alberto Quickly. *Quick Change*. Born: 1895. At liberty." The quiet bell sounded again.

"Hold on," I said. I felt myself murmuring. "Pictures, mirrors, and now here's a guy, Bradford, who is *all* women. And then here's another guy, Quickly, who is all men, every man." The bell faded. "Did Constance know them?"

Like a sleepwalker I moved to pick up Constance's Book of the Dead.

There it was.

Bradford on one page, near the beginning of the book.

Quickly toward the end.

"But no red circles around the names. So? Are they alive or dead?"

"Why not go see," said Henry.

Lightning struck. The lights failed again.

In the dark, Henry said, "Don't tell me, let me guess."

CHAPTER THIRTY-FOUR

CRUMLEY dropped us by the old apartment house and ran.

"Now," said Henry, "what are we doing here?"

Inside, I glanced up the three-story stairwell. "Searching for Marlene Dietrich alive and well."

Before I even knocked on the door, I caught the perfume through the paneling. I sneezed and knocked.

"Dear God," a voice said. "I haven't a thing to wear."

The door opened and a billowing butterfly kimono stood there with a Victorian relic inside, squirming to make it fit. It stopped squirming and tape-measured my shoes, my knee bones, my shoulders, and finally eye to eye.

"J. Wallington Bradford?" I cleared my throat. "Mr. Bradford?"

"Who's asking?" the creature in the doorway wondered. "Jesus. Come in. Come in. And who's this other thing?"

"I'm the boy's Seeing Eye." Henry probed the air. "That a chair? Think I'll sit. Sure smells strong in here. Nothing personal."

The kimono let loose a blizzard of confetti in its lungs and waved us in with a grand sweep of its sleeve. "I hope it isn't business that brings you here. Sit, while Mama pours gin. Big or small?"

Before I could speak he had filled a big glass with clear Bombay blue crystal liquor. I sipped.

"That's a good boy," said Bradford. "You staying five minutes or the night? My God, he's blushing. Is this about Rattigan?"

"Rattigan!" I cried. "How'd you know?"

"She was here and gone. Every few years Rattigan vanishes. It's how she divorces a new husband, an old lover, God, or her astrologer. *¿Quién sabe?*"

I nodded, stunned.

"She came years ago, asking how I did it. All those people, she said. Constance, I said, how many cat lives have *you* had? A thousand? Don't ask which flue I slid up, which bed I ran under!"

"But—"

"No buts. Mother Earth knows all. Constance invented Freud, tossed in Jung and Darwin. Did you know she bedded all six studio heads? It was a bet she took at the Brown Derby from Harry Cohn. 'I'll harvest Jack Warner and his brothers till their ears fly off,' she said.

"'All in the *same* year?' Cohn yelled.

"'Year, hell,' said Constance. 'In one week, with Sunday off!'

" 'I bet a hundred you can't!' said Cohn.

" 'Make it a thousand and you're on,' said Constance.

"Harry Cohn glared. 'What will you put up as collateral?'

" 'Me,' said Rattigan.

" 'Shake!' cried Cohn.

"She shook all over. 'Hold these!' She flung her pants in Cohn's lap and fled."

Breathless, J. W. Bradford raved on: "Did you know that once I was Judy Garland. Then Joan Crawford, then Bette Davis. I was Bankhead in *Lifeboat*. A real nightwalker, late sleeper, bed buster. You need help finding Rattigan? I can list her discards. Some fell in my lap. You want to *say* something?"

"Is there a *real* you in there, somewhere?" I said.

"God, I hope not. How terrible to find me in bed with just me! Rattigan. You tried her beach house? Artie Shaw stayed there after Caruso. She got *him* when she was thirteen. Drove him up the La Scala wall. When she topped off Lawrence Tibbett, he sang soprano. They had a squad car of paramedics by her joint, 1936, when she mouth-to-mouth breathed Thalberg into Forest Lawn. You okay?"

"I just got hit by a ten-ton safe."

"Take more gin. Tallulah says so."

"You'll help us find Constance?"

"No one else can. I loaned her my whole wardrobe a million years back. Gave her my makeup-box rejects, taught her perfumes, how to surprise her eyebrows, lift her ears, shorten her upper lip, widen her smile, flatten or bulge her bosom, walk taller than tall, or fall short. I was a mirror she posed in front of, watching me stare, blink, pretend remorse, alert, despair, delight, sing in a gilded cage, power-dive into pajamas, breaststroke out. She trotted in a high school pony, swarmed out a nest of ballerinas. By the time she left, she was someone else. That was ten thousand vaudevilles ago. And all so she could compete with other actresses for other roles in films, or maybe steal their men.

"Okay, doll," J. W. Bradford said as he scribbled on a pad. "Here's more names of those who loved Constance. Nine producers, ten directors, forty-five at-liberty actors, and a partridge in a pear tree."

"Did she never hold still?"

"Ever see those seals in Rattigan's surf? Slick as oil, quicker than quicksilver, hit the bed like lightning. Number one in the L.A. Marathon long before there was one. Could have been board chairman at three studios, but wound up as Vampira, Madame Defarge, and Dolley Madison. There!"

"Thanks." I scanned a list that would have filled the Bastille twice over.

"Now if you'll forgive, Mata Hari must *change!*"

Zip! He flourished his kimono.

Zip! I grabbed Henry's arm and we flew down the stairs and out onto the street.

"Hey!" someone cried. "Wait!"

I turned and looked up. Jean Harlow-Dietrich-Colbert

leaned over the top rail, smiling wildly, waiting for Von Stroheim to shoot her close-up.

"There's someone else like me, even crazier. Quickly!"

"Alberto Quickly!" I called. "He's alive?"

"He does one nightclub a week, then hospital rehabs. When they sew him up he repeats his farewell tour. Damn fool, in his nineties, said he found Constance (a lie!) on Route 66 when he was, my God, forty, fifty. Driving across country, he picked up this tomboy with suspicious breasts. Made her a star while his act faded. Runs a *théâtre intime* in his parlor. Charges folks on Friday nights to see Caesar stabbed, Antony on his sword, Cleopatra bitten." A piece of paper sailed down. "There! And something *else!*"

"What?"

"Connie, Helen, Annette, Roberta. Constance didn't show up for more lessons in changing lives! Last week. She was supposed to come back and didn't."

"I don't understand," I yelled.

"I had taught her things, dark, light, loud, soft, wild, quiet, some sort of new role she was looking for. She was coming back to me to learn some more. She wanted to be a new person. Maybe like her old self. But I didn't know how to help. Role-playing, Jesus, how do you get actors unhooked? W. C. Fields learned to be W. C. Fields in vaudeville. He never escaped those handcuffs. So here was Constance saying 'Help me to find a new self.' I said, 'Constance, I don't know how to help you. Get a priest to put a new skin around you.' "

A great bell rang in my head. Priest.

"Well, that's it," said Jean Harlow. "Did I confuse but amuse? Ciao." Bradford vanished.

"Quickly," I gasped. "Let's call Crumley."

"What's the rush?" said Henry.

"No, no, Alberto Quickly, the rabbit in and out of the hat, Hamlet's father's ghost."

"Oh, *him*," said Henry.

CHAPTER THIRTY-FIVE

WE dropped Henry off at some nice soft-spoken relatives on Central Avenue and then Crumley delivered me to the home of Alberto Quickly, ninety-nine years old, Rattigan's first "teacher."

"The first," he said. "The Bertillion expert, who finger-printed Constance toenail to elbow to knees."

In vaudeville he had been known as Mr. Metaphor, who acted all of *Old Curiosity Shop* or every last one of Fagin's brood in *Oliver Twist* as audiences cried "Mercy." He was more morbid than Marley, paler than Poe.

Quickly, the critics cried, orchestrated requiems to flood the Thames with mournful tides when, as Tosca, he flung himself into forever.

All this Metaphor-Quickly said glibly, happily, as I sat in his small theater-stage parlor. I waved away the box of

Kleenex he offered before he treated me to his Lucia, mad again.

"Stop," I cried at last. "What about Constance?"

"Hardly knew her," he said, "but I *did* know Katy Kelleher, 1926, my first Pygmalion child!"

"Pygmalion?" I murmured, pieces falling into place.

"Do you recall Molly Callahan, 1927?"

"Faintly."

"How about Polly Riordan, 1926?"

"Almost."

"Katy was Alice in Wonderland, Molly was Molly in *Mad Molly O'Day*. Polly was *Polly of the Circus,* same year. Katy, Molly, Polly—all Constance. A whirlwind blew in nameless, blew out famous. I taught her to shout, 'I'm Polly!' Producers cried, 'You are, you are!' The film was shot in six days. Then I revamped her to jump down Leo the Lion's throat. 'I'm Pretty Katy Kelly.' 'You are!' the lion pride yelled. Her second film done in four days! Kelly vanished, then Molly climbed the RKO radio tower. So it was Molly, Polly, Dolly, Sally, Gerty, Connie . . . and *Constance* rabbiting studio lawns!"

"No one ever guessed Constance played more than one part over the years?"

"Only I, Alberto Quickly, helped her to grab onto fame, fortune, and fondling! The golden greased pig! No one ever knew that some of the marquee names on Hollywood Boulevard were names Constance made up or borrowed. Could be she shuffled her tootsies in Grauman's forecourt with four different shoe sizes!"

"And where is Molly, Polly, Sally, Gerty, Connie, now?"

"Even *she* doesn't know. Here are six different addresses in twelve different summers. Maybe she drowned in deep grass. *Years* are a great hiding place. God hides you. Duck! What's my name?!"

He did a flip-flop cartwheel across the room. I heard his old bones scream.

"Ta-ta!" He grinned in pain.

"Mr. Metaphor!"

"You got it!" He dropped cold.

I leaned over him, terrified. He popped one eye wide.

"That was a *close* one. Prop me up. I scared Rattigan so, she ran." He babbled on. "It was only fitting. After all, I'm Fagin, Marley, Scrooge, Hamlet, Quickly. Someone like me had to be curious and try to figure out what year she lived in, or if she ever existed at all. The older I got, the more jealous I became of the gain and loss of Constance. I waited too long over the years, just as Hamlet waited too long to slay the foul fiend who killed his father's ghost! Ophelia and Caesar begged for slaughter. The memory of Constance summoned bull stampedes. So when I turned ninety all my voices raved for revenge. Like a damn fool I sent her the Book of the Dead. So it must be that Constance ran from my madness.

"Call an ambulance," Mr. Metaphor added. "I've got two broken tibias and a herniated groin. Did you write all that down?"

"Later."

"Don't wait! Write it. An hour from now I'll be in Valhalla harassing the statues. Where's my bed?"

I put him to bed.

"Slow down," I said. "That Book of the Dead, you say *you* sent that to Constance?"

"There was a half-ass semi–garage sale of actors' junk at the Film Ladies' League last month. I got some Fairbanks photos and a Crosby song sheet, and there, by God, was Rattigan's thrown-away phonebook stuffed with all her cat-litter-box lovers. My God, I was the snake in the garden. Grabbed onto damnation for a dime, eyed the lists, drank the poison. Why not give Rattigan bad dreams? Tracked her down, dropped the Dead Book, ran. *Did* it scare the stuffings out of her?"

"Oh, my God, it did." I stared into Mr. Quickly's grinning face. "Then you didn't have anything to do with that poor old soul lost on Mount Lowe?"

"Constance's first sucker? That stupid old guy is dead?"

"Newspapers killed him."

"Critics do that."

"No. Tons of old *Tribune*s fell on him."

"One way or the other, they kill."

"And you didn't harass Queen Califia?"

"That old Noah's Ark, two of every kind of lie in her. High/low, hot/cold. Camel dung and horse puckies. She told Constance where to go and she went. She dead, too?"

"Fell downstairs."

"*I* didn't trip her."

"Then there was the priest . . ."

"Her brother? Same mistake. Califia told her where to go. But he, my God, told her to go to hell. So Constance went. What killed *him?* God, everyone's dead!"

"She yelled at him. Or I think it was she."

"You know what she yelled?"

"No."

"*I* do."

"You?"

"Middle of the night, last night, I heard voices, thought I was dreaming. That voice, it had to be her. Maybe what she yelled at that poor damn priest, she yelled at me. Wanna hear?"

"I'm waiting."

"Oh, yeah. She yelled, 'How do I get back, where's the next place, how do I get back?'"

"Get back to where?"

There was a quick spin of thought behind Quickly's eyelids. He snorted.

"Her brother told her where to go and she went. And at last she said, 'I'm lost, show me the way.' Constance wants to be found. That *it?*"

"Yes. No. God, I don't know."

"Neither does she. Maybe that's why she yelled. But my house is built of bricks. It never fell."

"Others did."

"Her old husband, Califia, her brother?"

"It's a long story."

"And you have miles to go before you sleep?"

"Yeah."

"Don't wind up like this old mad hen that lays eggs any color you place me on. Red scarf. Red eggs. Blue rug. Blue. Purple camisole. Purple. That's me. Notice the plaid sheet here?"

It was all white and I told him so.

"You got bad eyes." He surveyed me. "You sure talk a lot. I'm pooped. Bye." And he slammed his eyes shut.

"Sir," I said.

"I'm busy," he murmured. "What's my name?"

"Fagin, Othello, Lear, O'Casey, Booth, Scrooge."

"Oh, yeah."

And then he snored.

CHAPTER THIRTY-SIX

I TAXIED out to the sea, back to my little place. I needed to think.

And then: there was a blow against my oceanfront door like a sledgehammer. *Wham!*

I jumped to get it before it fell in.

A flash of light blinded me from a single bright round crystal tucked in a mean eye.

"Hello, Edgar Wallace, you stupid goddamn son of a bitch, you!" a voice cried.

I fell back, aghast that he would call me Edgar Wallace, that dime-a-dance el cheapo hack!

"Hello, Fritz," I yelled, "you stupid goddamn son of a bitch, you! Come in!"

"I am!"

As if wearing heavy military boots, Fritz Wong clubbed the carpet. His heels cracked as he seized his monocle to hold it in the air and focus on me. "You're getting old!" he cried with relish.

"You already *are!*" I cried.

"Insults?"

"You get what you give!"

"Voice down, please."

"You first!" I yelled. "You *hear* what you called me?"

"Is Mickey Spillane better?"

"Out!"

"John Steinbeck?"

"Okay! Lower your voice."

"Is this okay?" he whispered.

"I can still hear you."

Fritz Wong barked a great laugh.

"That's my good bastard son."

"That's my two-timing illegitimate pa!"

We embraced with arms of steel in paroxysms of laughter.

Fritz Wong wiped his eyes. "Now that we've done the formalities," he rumbled. "How *are* you?"

"Alive. You?"

"Barely. Why the delay in delivering provender?"

I brought out Crumley's beer.

"Pig swill," said Fritz. "No wine? But . . ." He drank deep and grimaced. "Now." He sat down heavily in my only chair. "How can I help?"

"What makes you think I need help?"

"You always *will!* Wait! I can't stand this." He stomped out into the rain and lunged back with a bottle of Le Corton, which, silently, he opened with a fancy bright silver corkscrew that he pulled from his pocket.

I brought out two old but clean jelly jars. Fritz eyed them with scorn as he poured.

"1949!" he said. "A *great* year. I expect loud exclamations!"

I drank.

"Don't chugalug!" Fritz shouted. "For Christ's sake, inhale! Breathe!"

I inhaled. I swirled the wine. "Pretty good."

"Jesus Christ! Good?"

"Let me think."

"Goddammit. Don't *think!* Drink with your nose! Exhale through your ears!"

He showed me how, eyes shut.

I did the same. "Excellent."

"Now sit down and shut up."

"This is *my* place, Fritz."

"Not now it isn't."

I sat on the floor, leaning against the wall, and he stood over me like Caesar astride an ant farm.

"Now," he said, "spill the beans."

I lined them up and spilled them.

When I finished, Fritz refilled my jelly glass reluctantly.

"You don't deserve this," he muttered, "but yours was a fair performance drinking the vintage. Shut up. Sip."

"If anyone can solve Rattigan," he said, sipping, "it's me. Or should I say, I? Quiet."

He opened the front door on the lovely endless rain. "You like this?"

"Love it."

"Sap!" Fritz screwed his monocle in for a long glance up-shore.

"Rattigan's place up there, eh? Not home for seven days? Maybe dead? Empress of the killing ground, yes, but she will never be caught dead. One day she will simply disappear and no one will know what happened. Now, shall I spill my beans?"

He poured the last of the Le Corton, hating the jelly glass, loving the wine.

He was at liberty, he said, unemployed. No films for two years. Too old, they said.

"I'm the youngest acrobat in any bed on three continents!" he protested. "Now I have got my hands on Bernard Shaw's play *Saint Joan*. But how do you cast that incredible play? So, meanwhile I have a Jules Verne novel in the public domain, free and clear, with a dumb-cluck fly-by-night producer who says nothing and steals much, so I need a second-rate science-fiction writer—you—to work for scale on this half-ass masterwork. Say yes."

Before I could speak . . .

There was a huge deluge of rain and a crack of fire and thunder, during which Fritz barked: "You're *hired!* Now. Do you have more to show and tell?"

I showed and told.

The photos clipped from the ancient newspapers and Scotch-taped on the wall over my bed. Fritz had to half lie down, cursing, to look at the damned things.

"With *one* eye, the other destroyed in a duel—"

"A duel?" I exclaimed. "You never said—"

"Shut up and read the names under the pictures to the Cyclops German director."

I read the names.

Fritz repeated them.

"Yes, I remember her." He reached to touch. "And that one. And, yes, this one. My God, what a rogues' gallery."

"Did you work with all or some?"

"Some I did two falls out of three in a Santa Barbara motel. I do not brag. A thing is either true or not."

"You've never lied to me, Fritz."

"I have, but you were too stupid to see. Polly. Molly. Dolly. Sounds like a cheap Swiss bell ringers' act. Hold on. Can't be. Maybe. Yes!"

He was leaning up, adjusting his monocle, squinting hard. "Why didn't I see? Dummkopf. But there was time between. Years. That one and that one, and that. Good God!"

"What, Fritz?"

"They're all the same actress, the same woman. Different hair, different hairdo, different color, different makeup. Thick eyebrows, thin eyebrows, no eyebrows. Small lips, large lips. Eyelashes, no eyelashes. Women's tricks. Woman came up to me last week on Hollywood Boulevard and said, 'Do you know me?' 'No,' I said. 'I'm so-and-so,' she said. I studied her nose. Nose job. Looked at her mouth. Mouth job. Eyebrows? New eyebrows. Plus, she had lost thirty pounds and turned blond. How in hell was I supposed to know who she was?

"These pictures, where did you get them?"

"Up on Mount Lowe—"

"That dumb newspaper librarian. I went up there once to do research. Quit. Couldn't breathe in all those goddamn news stacks. Call me, I yelled, when you have a clearance! Constance's dimwit first husband, married when she rebounded off a manslaughter bomb scare. How I managed to direct her in at least three films and never guessed at her changes! Christ! An imp inside a devil inside Lucifer's flesh-eating wife."

"Maybe because," I said, "you were courting Marlene Dietrich one of those years?"

"Courting? Is that what they call it?" Fritz barked a laugh and rocked off the edge of the bed. "Take those damn things down. If I can help, I'll need the junk."

"There's more like this," I said. "Grauman's Chinese, the old projection booth, the old—"

"That crummy lunatic?"

"I wouldn't say that."

"Why not! He had a missing reel of my UFA film *Atlantica*. I went to see. He tried to tie me to a chair and force-feed me old Rin Tin Tin serials. I threatened to jump off the balcony, so he let me go with *Atlantica*. So."

He spread the pictures out on the bed and gave them the fiery stare of his monocle.

"You say there are more pictures like these upstairs at Grauman's?"

"Yes," I said.

"Would you mind traveling ninety-five miles an hour in

an Alfa-Romeo to get to Grauman's Chinese in less than five minutes?"

The blood drained from my face.

"You would *not* mind," said Fritz.

He blundered swiftly out into the rain. His Alfa-Romeo was in full space-rocket throttle when I fell in.

CHAPTER THIRTY-SEVEN

"Flashlight, matches, pad and pencil should we need to leave a note." I checked my pockets.

"Wine," Fritz added, "in case the damn dogs up there on the cliff don't carry brandy."

We passed a bottle of wine between us as we scanned the avalanche of dark stairs leading to the old projection booth.

Fritz smiled. "Me first. If you fall I don't want to catch."

"Some friendship."

Fritz plowed the dark. I plowed after, swiveling the flashlight beam.

"Why are you helping me?" I gasped.

"I called Crumley. He said he's hiding all day in bed. Me, being around half-ass dimwits like you clears my blood and restarts my heart. Watch that flashlight, I might fall."

"Don't tempt me." I bobbed the light.

"I hate to say," Fritz said, "but you give as good as you get. You're my tenth bastard, out of Marie Dressler!"

We were higher now, in nosebleed territory.

We reached the top of the second balcony, Fritz raging at the altitude but happy to hear himself rage.

"Explain again," Fritz said as we continued climbing. "Up here. Then what?"

"Then we go as far down as we've come up. Basement mirror names. A glass catacomb."

"Knock," said Fritz, at last.

I knocked and the projection room door swung inward on dim lights from two projectors, one lit and working.

I swung my flash beam along the wall and sucked air.

"What?" said Fritz.

"They're gone!" I said. "The pictures. The walls have been stripped."

I played my flashlight beam along the empty spaces in dismay. All the dark-room "ghosts" had indeed vanished.

"Goddamn! Jesus! Christ!" I stopped and swore. "My God, I sound like you!"

"My son, my son," Fritz said, pleased. "Move the light!"

"Quiet." I inched forward, holding the beam unsteadily on what sat between the projectors.

It was Constance's father, of course, erect and cold, one hand touching a machine switch.

One projector was running full spin with a reel that looped through the projector lens and down, around, a spiral that repeated images again and again every ten seconds. The small door that could open to let the images shoot down to fill the theater screen was shut, so the images were trapped on the inside of the door, small, but if you bent close and squinted, you could see—

Sally, Dolly, Molly, Holly, Gaily, Nellie, Roby, Sally, Dolly, Molly—around about, on and on.

I studied old man Rattigan, frozen in place, and whether his grimace showed triumph or need, I could not say.

I glanced beyond to those walls now empty of Sally, Dolly, Molly, but whoever had seized them hadn't figured that the old man, seeing his "family" snatched, had switched on this loop to save the past. Or—

My mind sank.

I heard Betty Kelly's voice shrieking what Constance had shrieked, *Forgive me, forgive me, forgive me.* And Quickly recalling, *How do I get it back, back, back?* Get what back? Her other self?

Did someone do this to you? I thought, standing over the old dead man. Or did you do it to yourself?

The dead man's white marble eyes were still.

I cut the projector.

All the faces still flowed on my retina, the dancing daughter, the butterfly, the Chinese vamp, the tomboy clown.

"Poor lost soul," I whispered.

"You *know* him?" said Fritz.

"No."

"Then he's no poor lost soul."

"Fritz! Did you ever have a heart?"

"Simple bypass. I had it removed."

"How do you live without it?"

"Because . . ." Fritz handed me his monocle. I fit the cold glass to my eye and stared.

"Because," he said, "I'm a—"

"Stupid goddamn son of a bitch?"

"Bull's-eye!" Fritz said.

"Let's go," he added. "This place is a morgue."

"Always *was*," I said.

I called Henry, and told him to take a taxi to Grauman's. Pronto.

CHAPTER THIRTY-EIGHT

BLIND Henry was waiting for us in an aisle leading down to the orchestra pit and from there to the hidden basement dressing rooms.

"Don't tell," Henry said.

"About what, Henry?"

"The pictures up in that projection booth. Kaput? That's Fritz Wong's lingo."

"The same to you," said Fritz.

"Henry, how'd you guess?"

"I knew." Henry fixed his sightless eyes down at the pit. "I just visited the mirrors. I don't need a cane, and sure as heck no flashlight. Just reached when I was there and touched the glass. That's how I knew the pictures upstairs had to be gone. Felt all along forty feet of glass. Clean. All scraped away. So . . ." He stared again at the sightless uphill seats. "Upstairs. All gone. Right?"

"Right." I exhaled, somewhat stunned.

"Let me show you." Henry turned to the pit.

"Wait, I've got my flash."

"When you going to learn?" Henry mocked, and stepped down into the pit in one silent motion.

I followed. Fritz glared at our parade.

"Well," I said, "what are you *waiting* for?"

Fritz moved.

CHAPTER THIRTY-NINE

"There." Henry pointed his nose at the long line of mirrors. "What did I say?"

I moved along the aisle of glass, touching with my flash and then my fingers.

"So?" Fritz growled.

"There were names and now no names, just like there were pictures and now no pictures."

"Told you," said Henry.

"How come the sightless are never the wordless?" said Fritz.

"Got to do something to fill the time. Shall I recite the names?"

I said the names from memory.

"You left out Carmen Carlotta," said Henry.

"Oh, yeah. Carlotta."

Fritz glanced up.

"And whoever swiped the pictures upstairs?"

"Cleaned and scraped the mirrors."

"So all those ladies are like they never was," said Henry.

He leaned in along the line of mirrors and gave a last brush with his blind fingertips to the glass here, there, and farther on down. "Yeah. Empty. Damn. Those names were caked on. Took lots to scrub it off. Who?"

"Henrietta, Mabel, Gloria, Lydia, Alice . . ."

"They all came down to clean up?"

"They did and they didn't. We've already said it, Henry, that all of those women came and went, were born and died, and wrote their names, like grave markers."

"So?"

"And those names were not written all at once. So starting back in the twenties, those women, ladies, whatever, came down here for their obsequies, a funeral of one. When they looked in their first mirror, they saw one face, and when they moved to the next, the face was changed."

"Now you're cooking."

"So, Henry, what's here is a grand parade of funerals, births, and burials, all done with the same two hands and one spade."

"But the scribbles"—Henry reached out to emptiness—"were different."

"People change. She couldn't make up her mind to one life or how to live it. So she stood in front of the mirror and wiped off her lipstick and painted another mouth, and washed off her eyebrows and painted better ones, or widened her eyes and raised her hairline and tilted her hat like a lampshade or took it off and threw it, or took off her dress and stood here starkers."

"Starkers." Henry smiled. "Now you got it."

"Hush," I said.

"That's work," Henry continued. "Scribbling those mirrors, looking to see how she changed."

"Didn't happen overnight. Once a year, maybe two years, and she'd show up with a smaller mouth or a thinner shape and liked what she saw and went away to become that person for half a year or just one summer. How's that, Henry?"

Henry moved his lips, whispering, "Constance."

"Sure," he murmured, "she never smelled the same way twice." Henry shuffled, touching the mirrors until he reached the open manhole. "I'm near, right?"

"One more step would do it, Henry."

We looked down at the round hole in the cement. From below came sounds of winds blowing in from San Fernando, Glendale, and who knows where else—Far Rockaway? The light rain runoff was sliding below, a mere trickle, hardly enough to cool your ankles.

"Dead end," said Henry. "Nothing upstairs, nothing down. Clues to somebody gone. But where?"

As if in answer, a most ungodly cry came from the dark hole in the cold floor. We all jumped.

"Jesus!" Fritz cried.

"Christ!" I yelled.

"Lord!" said Henry. "That can't be Molly, Dolly, Holly, can it?"

I repeated that rosary in silence.

Fritz read my lips and cursed.

The cry came again, farther away, being carried downstream. Tears exploded from my eyes. I jumped forward to sway over the manhole. Fritz grabbed my elbow.

"Did you hear?" I cried.

"Nothing!" said Fritz.

"That scream!"

"That's just the water," Fritz said.

"Fritz!"

"You calling me a *liar?*"

"Fritz!"

"The way you say Fritz, I lie. No lie. You don't really want to, hell, go down *there!* Godammit!"

"Let me go!"

"If your wife was here, she'd push you in, dummkopf!"

I stared at the open manhole. Far away there was another cry. Fritz cursed.

"You come with me," I said.

"No, no."

"You afraid?"

"Afraid?" Fritz plucked the monocle from his eye. It was like pulling the spigot on his blood. His suntan paled. His eye watered. "Afraid? Of a damn dark stupid underground cave, Fritz Wong?"

"Sorry," I said.

"Don't be sorry for the greatest UFA director in cinema history." He planted his fiery monocle back in its groove.

"Well, what now?" he demanded. "I find a phone and call Crumley to drag you out of this black hole? You goddamn teenage death-wisher!"

"I'm no teenager."

"No? Then why do I see crouched by that damn hole an Olympic chump high-diving into a tide half an inch deep? Go on, break your neck, drown in garbage!"

"Tell Crumley to drive into the storm drain and meet me halfway from the sea. If he sees Constance, grab her. If he finds me, grab even quicker."

Fritz shut one eye to target me with fire from the other, contempt under glass.

"You will take direction from an Academy Award–winning director?"

"What?"

"Drop quick. When you hit, don't stop. Whatever's down there can't grab you if you run! If you see her, tell her to try to catch up. 'Stood?"

" 'Stood!"

"Now die like a dog. Or . . ." he added, scowling, "live like a stoop who got the hell through."

"Meet you at the ocean?"

"I won't be there!"

"Oh yes you will!"

He lurched toward the basement door, and Henry.

"You want to follow that idiot?" he roared.

"No."

"You afraid of the dark?"

"I *am* the dark!" said Henry.

They were gone.

Cursing Germanic curses, I climbed down into mists, fogs, and rains of night.

CHAPTER FORTY

QUITE suddenly I was in Mexico, 1945. Rome, 1950.

Catacombs.

The thing about darkness is you can imagine, in one direction, wall-to-wall mummies torn from their graves because they couldn't pay the funeral rent.

Or kindling by the thousand-bone-piles, polo heads of skulls to be hammered downfield.

Darkness.

And me caught between ways that led to eternal twilights in Mexico, eternity beneath the Vatican.

Darkness.

I stared at the ladder leading up to safety—Blind Henry and angry Fritz. But they were long gone toward the light and the crazies out front of Grauman's.

I heard the surf pounding like a great heart, ten miles

downstream in Venice. There, hell, was safety. But twenty thousand yards of dim concrete floor stood between me and the salty night wind.

I gasped air because . . .

A pale man shambled out of the dark.

I don't mean he walked crazy-legs, but there was something about his whole frame, his knees and elbows, the way his head toppled or his hands flopped like shot birds. His stare froze me.

"I *know* you," he cried.

I dropped the flashlight.

He grabbed it and exclaimed, "What're *you* doing down here?" His voice knocked off the concrete walls. "Didn't you used to *be*—?" He said my name. "*Sure!* Jesus, you *hiding?* You down here to stay? Welcome, I guess." His pale shadow arm waved my flashlight. "Some place, eh? Been here horses' years. Came down to see. Never went back. Lotsa friends. Want to meet 'em?"

I shook my head.

He snorted. "Hell! Why *would* you want to meet these lost underground jerks?"

"How do you know my name?" I said. "Did we go to school together?"

"You *don't* remember? Hell and damn!"

"Harold?" I said. "Ross?"

There was just the drip of a lone faucet somewhere.

I added more names. Tears leaped to my eyes. Ralph, Sammy, Arnold, school chums. Gary, Philip, off to war, for God's sake.

"Who are you? When did I know you?"

"Nobody ever knows anyone," he said, backing off.

"Were you my best pal?"

"I always knew you'd get on. Always knew I'd get lost," he said, a mile away.

"The war."

"I died *before* the war. Died *after* it. I was never born, so how come?" Fading.

"Eddie! Ed. Edward. Eduardo, it's *got* to be!" My heart beat swiftly, my voice rose.

"When did you last call? Did you get around to my funeral? Did you even *know?*"

"I never knew," I said, inching closer.

"Come again. Don't knock. I'll always be here. Wait! You *searching* for someone?" he cried. "What's she *look* like? You *hear* that? What's *she* look like? Am I right? Yes, no?"

"Yes!" I blurted.

"She went that way." He waved my flash.

"When—?"

"Just now. What's she doing here in Dante's Inferno?"

"What did she look like?" I burst out.

"Chanel No. 5!"

"What?"

"Chanel! That'll bring the rats running. She'll be lucky if she makes it to the surf. 'Stay off Muscle Beach!' I yelled."

"What?"

"'Stay!' I yelled. She's here somewhere. Chanel No. 5!"

I seized my flash from his hands, turned it back on his ghost face.

"Where?"

"Why?" He laughed wildly.

"God, I don't know."

"This way, yeah, this way."

His laugh caromed in all directions.

"Hold on! I can't see!"

"You don't have to. Chanel!"

More laughter.

I swiveled my flash.

Now, as he babbled, I heard something like weather, a seasonal change, a distant rainfall. Dry wash, I thought, but not dry, a flash flood, this damned place ankle-deep, knee-deep, then drowned all the way to the sea!

I whipped my flashlight beam up, around, back. Nothing. The sound grew. More whispers coming, yes, not a change of season, dry weather becoming wet, but whispers of people, not rain on the channel floor but the slap of bare feet on cement, and the shuffled murmur of quiet discovery, arguments, curiosity.

People, I thought, my God, more shadows like this one, more voices, the whole damn clan, shadows and shadows of shadows, like the silent ghosts on Rattigan's ceiling, specters that flowed up, around, and vanished like rainfall.

But what if her film ghosts had blown free of her projector, and the pale screens up above in Grauman's, and the wind blew and the phantoms caught cobwebs and light and found voices, what if, dear God, what if?

Stupid! I cut the light, for the rain-channel-crazed man was still mumbling and yammering close. I felt his hot breath on my cheek and I lurched back, afraid to light his face, afraid to sluice the channel a second time to freeze the floodwater of ghost voices, for they were louder now, closer. The dark flowed, the unseen crowd gathered, as this crazed fool grew taller, nearer, and I felt a plucking at my sleeves to seize, hold, bind, and the rainfall voices far off blew nearer and I knew that I should get, go, run like hell and hope they were all legless wonders!

"I—" I bleated.

"What's wrong?" my friend cried.

"I—"

"Why are you afraid? Look. Look! Look there!"

And I was thrust and bumped through darkness to a greater mass of darkness, which was a cluster of shadows and then flesh. A crowd gathered around a shape that wept and lamented and yearned and it was the sound of a woman drowning in darkness.

As the woman moaned and cried and wept and grew silent to mourn again, I edged near.

And then someone thought to hold out a cigarette lighter, clicking it so that the small blue flame extended toward a shawled and unkempt creature, that fretting soul.

Inspired, another lighter drifted out of the night, hissing, and breathed light to hold steady. And then another and another, small flame after flame, like so many fireflies gathered in a circle until there was illumination circling steadily. And floating within to reveal that misery, that exaltation, that whispering, that sobbing, that voice of sudden pronouncements, were six, twelve, twenty more small blue fires, thrust and held to ignite the voice, to give it a shape, to shine the mystery. The more firefly lights, the higher the voice shrilled, asking for some unseen gift, recognition, asking for attention, demanding to live, asking to solve that form, face, and presence.

"Only from my voices, I would lose all heart!" she lamented.

What? I thought. What's that? Familiar! I almost guessed. Almost knew. What?

"The bells came down from heaven and their echoes linger in the fields. Through the quiet of the countryside, my voices!" she cried.

What? Almost! Familiar, I thought. Oh God, what?

Then a thunderous flood of storm wind flashed from the far sea, drenched with salt odor and a smash of thunder.

"You!" I cried. "You!"

And all the fires blew out to screams in utter darkness.

I called her name, but the only answer was a torrent of shouts in an avalanche of feet in full stampede.

In the roar and rush and ranting, some soft flesh struck my arm, my face, my knee, and then it was gone as I cried, "You!" and "You!" again.

There was an immense roundabout, a thousand millraces of darkness from which a single flame ignited near my mouth and one of the strange beasts cursed, seeing me, and shouted, "You, you scared her away! You!"

And hands were thrust to snatch at me until I fell back.

"No!" I turned and leaped, hoping to hell it was toward the sea and not the ghosts.

I stumbled and fell. My flashlight skittered. Christ, I thought, if I can't get it back—!

I scrambled on hands and knees.

"Oh, please, *please!*"

And my fingers closed on the flashlight, which resurrected my flesh, got me upright, swaying with the black flood behind, and I broke into a drunken run. Don't fall, I thought, hold the light like a rope to pull you, don't fall, don't look back! Are they close, are they near, are there others waiting? Great God!

At which moment the most glorious sound cracked the channel. There was an illumination ahead like the sunrise at heaven's door, a loud chant of car horn, an avalanche of thunder! A car.

People like me think in film-bit flashes, over in an instant, dumb in retrospect, but a lightning bolt of exhilaration. John Ford, I thought, Monument Valley! Indians! But now, the damn cavalry!

For ahead, in full plunge from the sea . . .

My salvation, an old wreck.

And half standing up front . . . Crumley.

Yelling the worst curses he had ever yelled, cursing me with the foulest curses ever, but glad he had found me and then cursing this damn fool again.

"Don't kill me!" I cried.

The car braked near my feet.

"Not till we get *outta* here!" Crumley shrieked.

The darkness, lit by headlights, reared back. I was frozen with Crumley blaring the horn, waving arms, spitting teeth, going blind.

"You're lucky this damn buggy made it in! What *gives?*"

I stared back into the darkness.

"Nothing."

"Then you won't be needing a lift!" Crumley gunned the gas.

I jumped in and landed so hard the jalopy shook.

Crumley grabbed my chin. "You okay?"

"Now, yes!"

"We gotta back out!"

"Back out!" I cried. The shadows loomed. "At fifty miles an hour?"

"Sixty!"

Crumley glared at the night.

"Satchel Paige said don't look back. Something may be gaining on you."

A dozen figures lurched into the light.

"Now!" I yelled.

We left . . .

At seventy miles an hour, backward.

Crumley yelled, "Henry called, said where the damn dumb stupid Martian was!"

"Henry," I gasped.

"Fritz called! Said you were twice as stupid as Henry said!"

"I am! Faster!"

Faster.

I could hear the surf.

CHAPTER FORTY-ONE

WE motored out of the storm drain and I looked south one hundred yards and gasped. "Ohmigod, look!"

Crumley looked.

"There's Rattigan's place, two hundred feet away. How come we never noticed the storm drain came out so close?"

"We never used the storm drain before as Route 66."

"So if we could take it from Grauman's Chinese all the way here, Constance could have gone from here to Grauman's."

"Only if she was nuts. Hell. She was a Brazilian nut factory. Look."

There were a dozen narrow swerving marks in the sand. "Bicycle tracks. Bike it in one hour, tops."

"God, no, I don't see her on a bike."

I stood up in the jalopy to peer back at the tunnel.

"She's there. I doubt she's moved. She's still in there, going somewhere else, not here. Poor Constance."

"Poor?" Crumley erupted. "Tough as a rhino. Keep belly-aching about that five-and-dime floozy, I'll phone your wife to come crack your dog biscuits!"

"I haven't done anything wrong."

"No?" Crumley gunned the car the rest of the way out on the shore. "Three days of maniac running in and out of lousy L.A. palmistry parlors, upstairs Chinese balconies, climbing Mount Lowe! A parade of losers, all because of an A-1 skirt who gets the Oscar for loss-leading. *Wrong?* Rip the roll from my pianola if I've played the wrong tune!"

"Crumley! In that storm drain, I think I saw her. Could I just say 'go to hell'?"

"Sure!"

"Liar," I said. "You drink vodka, pee apple juice. I've got your number."

Crumley gunned the motor. "What're you getting at?"

"You're an altar boy."

"Christ, let me move this wreck out front of that damn fool sailor's delight!"

He drove fast, then slow, eyes half-shut, teeth gritted. "Well?"

I swallowed hard and said, "You're a boy soprano. You made your dad and mom proud at midnight mass. Hell, I've seen the ghost under your skin, in movies where you pretended your eyes weren't wet. A Catholic camel with a broken back. Great sinners, Crum, make great saints. No one's so bad they don't deserve a second chance."

"Rattigan's had ninety!"

"Would Jesus have kept count?"

"Damn, yes!"

"No, because some far-off late night, you'll call a priest to bless you and he'll carry you back to some Christmas night when your dad was proud and your ma cried and as you shut your eyes you'll be so damned glad to be home again you won't have to go pee to hide your tears. You still haven't given up hope. Know why?"

"Why, dammit?"

"Because *I* want it for you, Crum. Want you to be happy, want you to come home to something, anything, before it's too late. Let me tell you a story—"

"Why are you blabbing at a time like this? You just barely got away from a tribe of lunatics. What *did* you see in that flood channel?"

"I don't know, I'm not sure."

"Ohmigod, wait!" Crumley rummaged in the glove compartment and with a cry of relief uncorked a small flask and drank. "If I have to sit here with the tide going out and your hot air rising—speak."

I spoke: "When I was twelve a carnival magician, Mr. Electrico, came to my hometown. He touched me with his flaming sword and yelled, 'Live forever!' Why did he tell me that, Crumley? Was there something in my face, the way I acted, stood, sat, talked, what? All I know is somehow, burning me with his great eyes, he gave me my future. Leaving the carnival, I stood by the carousel, heard the calliope playing 'Beautiful Ohio,' and I wept. I knew something incredible had happened, something wonderful and nameless. Within three weeks, twelve years old, I started to write. I have written every day since. How come, Crumley, how come?"

"Here," said Crumley. "Finish this."

I drank the rest of the vodka.

"How come?" I said quietly again.

Now it was Crumley's turn: "Because he saw you were a romantic sap, a Dumpster for magic, a cloud-walker who found shadows on ceilings and said they were real. Christ, I don't know. You always look like you've just showered even if you rolled in dog doo. I can't stand all your innocence. Maybe that's what Electrico saw. Where's that vodka? Oh yeah, gone. You done?"

"No," I said. "Since Mr. Electrico pointed me in the right direction, shouldn't I pay back? Do I keep Mr. Electrico to myself, or let him help me save her?"

"Psychic crap!"

"Hunches. I don't know any other way to live. When I got married friends warned Maggie I wasn't going anywhere. I said, 'I'm going to the Moon and Mars, want to come along?' And she said yes. So far, it hasn't been so bad, has it? And on your way to a 'bless me, Father,' and a happy death, can't you find it in your heart to bring Rattigan?"

Crumley stared straight ahead.

"You mean all that?"

He reached over and touched under my eyes and brought his fingers back to his tongue.

"The real stuff," he murmured. "Salt. Your wife said you cry at phone books," he said quietly.

"Phone books full of people lost in graveyards, maybe. If I quit now, I'd never forgive myself. Or you, if you made me stop."

After a long moment Crumley shifted out of the car. "Wait," he said, not looking at me. "I got to go pee."

CHAPTER FORTY-TWO

HE came back after a long while.

"You sure know how to hurt a guy," he said as he climbed back into the jalopy.

"Just stir, don't shake."

Crumley cocked his head at me. "You're a queer egg."

"You're another."

We drove slowly along the shore toward Rattigan's. I was silent.

"You got another hairball?" Crumley said.

"Why is it," I said, "someone like Constance is a lightning bolt, performing seal, high-wire frolicker, wild laughing human, and at the same time she's the devil incarnate, an evil cheater at life's loaded deck?"

"Go ask Alexander the Great," said Crumley. "Look at Attila the Hun, who loved dogs; Hitler, too. Bone up on

Stalin, Lenin, Mussolini, Mao, hell's Anvil Chorus. Rommel, good family man. How do you cradle cats and cut throats, bake cookies *and* people? How come we love Richard the Third, who dumped kids in wine casks? How come TV is all Al Capone reruns? God won't say."

"I don't ask. He turned us loose. It's up to us, once He took off the leash. Who wrote, 'Malt does more than Milton can, to justify God's way towards Man?' I rewrote it and added, 'And Freud spoils kids and spares the rod, to justify Man's ways toward God.'"

Crumley snorted. "Freud was a nut loose in a fruit patch. I always believed smart-ass punks need their teeth punched."

"My dad never broke my teeth."

"That's because you're a half-stale Christmas fruitcake, the kind no one eats."

"But Constance is *beautiful!*"

"You mistake energy for beauty. Overseas, French girls knocked me flat. They blink, wave, dance, stand on their heads to prove they're alive. Hell, Constance is all battery acid and short circuit. If she ever slows down she'll get—"

"Ugly? No!"

"Gimme those!" He seized the glasses off my nose and peered through them.

"Rose-colored! How do things look *without* them?"

"Nothing's there."

"Great! There's not much worth seeing!"

"There's Paris in the spring. Paris in the rain. Paris on New Year's Eve."

"You *been* there?"

"I saw the movies. Paris. Gimme."

"I'll just keep these until you take waltz lessons from blind Henry." Crumley shoved my glasses in his pocket.

As we pulled our jalopy up on the shore in front of the white château, we saw two dark shapes by her oceanside pool, under the umbrella, to keep off the moonlight.

Crumley and I trudged up the dune and peered in at Blind Henry and angry Fritz Wong. There were martinis laid out on a tray.

"I knew," Henry said, "after that storm drain you'd seek refreshment. Grab. Drink."

We grabbed and drank.

Fritz soaked his monocle in vodka, thrust it in his stare, and said, "That's better!" And then he finished the drink.

CHAPTER FORTY-THREE

I WENT 'round, placing camp chairs by the pool.

Crumley watched with a dour eye and said, "Let me guess. This is the finale of an Agatha Christie murder mystery, and Poirot's got all the usual suspects stashed poolside."

"Bull's-eye."

"Proceed."

I proceeded.

"This chair here is for the Mount Lowe collector of old newspapers."

"Who will testify in absentia?"

"In absentia. This next chair is for Queen Califia, long gone, with her palmistry and head bumps."

I kept moving. "Third chair: Father Rattigan. Fourth chair: Grauman's Chinese mile-high projectionist. Fifth chair: J. W. Bradford, a.k.a. Tallulah, Garbo, Swanson,

Colbert. Sixth: Professor Quickly, a.k.a. Scrooge, Nicholas Nickleby, Richard the Third. Seventh chair: me. Eighth chair: Constance."

"Hold on."

Crumley got up and pinned his badge on my shirt.

"We going to sit here," said Fritz, "and listen to a fourth-rate Nancy Drew—"

"Stash your monocle," said Crumley.

Fritz stashed his monocle.

"Now," said Crumley, "junior?"

Junior moved behind the chairs.

"For starters, I'm Rattigan running in the rain with two Books of the Dead. Some already dead, some about to die."

I laid the two books on the glass-top table.

"We all know now that Quickly, in a spurt of nostalgic madness, sent the one book, with all the dead people, to frighten Constance. She came running from her past, her memories of a fast, furious, and destructive life."

"You can say that again," said Crumley.

I waited.

"Sorry," said Crumley.

I picked up the second book, Constance's more personal, recent phone lists.

"But what if Constance, hit by the old Book of the Dead, got wired back into her griefs, her losses in that past, and decided, in order to make do with it, she had to destroy it, person by person, one by one. What if she red-lined the names and forgot she had done it?"

"What if?" Crumley sighed.

"Let the idiot express his delight." Fritz Wong tucked his monocle back in his eye and leaned forward. "So the Rattigan goes to kill, maim, or at least threaten her own past, *ja?*" he said with heavy Germanic concern.

"Is that the way the next scene plays?" I asked.

"Action," said Fritz, amused.

I swayed behind the first empty chair.

"Here we are at the dead end of the old trolley-tram line on Mount Lowe."

Fritz and Crumley nodded, seeing the mummy there, wrapped in headlines.

"Wait." Blind Henry squinted. "Okay, I'm there."

"Her first husband is there, her first big mistake. So she goes up to swipe the newspapers with all her old selves filed away. She grabs the papers, like I did, and gives a final yell. Whether she pushed the landslide of newsprint, or gave one last shriek, who knows? Regardless, the Mount Lowe trolley master drowned in a bad-news avalanche. Okay?"

I looked over at Crumley, whose mouth gaped with his "okay." He nodded, as did Fritz. Henry sensed this and gave the go-ahead.

"Chair number two. Bunker Hill. Queen Califia. Predictor of futures, insurer of fates."

I held on to the chair as if I pushed that massive elephant on roller skates.

"Constance shouted outside her door. Califia wasn't murdered any more than that Mount Lowe Egyptian relic was. Yelled at, sure, by Rattigan, telling Califia to take back all her lousy predictions that *insured* the future. Califia had unrolled a papyrus road map, Constance followed, blind as a bat—sorry, Henry—all enthusiasm. Would Califia lie? No! Was the future wondrous? You betcha! Now, late in the game, Constance wanted retractions. Califia would have retracted, told new lies, and gone on living, but alarmed, fell downstairs into her grave. Not murder, but panic."

"So much for Califia," said Crumley, trying to hide his approval.

"Scene three, take one," said Fritz.

"Scene three, take one, chair number three." I moved. "This here is the confessional booth, St. Vibiana's."

Fritz scooched his chair closer, his monocle a lighthouse flash, searching my small private stage. He chopped his head at me to continue.

"And here's Rattigan's bighearted brother, trying to lead her along the straight and narrow. When Califia said 'left,' he yelled 'right,' and maybe after years of storms of brutal sin, he threw up his hands, tossed her out of the church. But she came back, raving, demanding absolution, screaming her demands, purify me, forgive me, your own flesh, give way, give in, but he clapped his hands over his ears and yelled against her yell, and his yells, not hers, struck him dead."

"So you say," said Fritz, one eye shut, the fire from his monocle stabbing. "Prove it. If we're going to shoot this like a goddamn film, write me the moment of truth. Tell how you *know* the priest killed himself with his own rage, yes?"

"Who the hell's the detective here?" Crumley cut in.

"The boy wonder is," drawled Fritz, not looking at him,

still shooting lightning bolts of optical glass at me. "He gets hired or fired by what he next claims."

"I'm not applying for a job," I said.

"You've already got it," said Fritz. "Or get thrown out on your ass. I'm the studio head and you're plea-bargaining. How do you know the priest was self-murdered?"

I exhaled.

"Because I heard him breathe, watched his face, saw him run. He couldn't stand Constance diving in the surf one way, to come out another. She was hot desert air, he was fog. Collision. Lightning. Bodies."

"All from one priest and one bad sister?"

"Saint. Sinner," I said.

Fritz Wong stiffened with a glow in his face and a most ungodly smile.

"You got the job. Crumley?"

Crumley reared back from Fritz but at last nodded. "As proof? It'll do. Next?"

I moved on to the next chair.

"Here we are at Grauman's Chinese, up high, late night, film running, figures on the screen, pictures on the wall. All of Rattigan's former selves nailed, ready to be nabbed. And the one man who really knows her, bum to belly button, her dad, keeper of the unholy flame, but he doesn't want her either, so she busts in and swipes the pictures that prove her past. She's got to burn those, too, because she doesn't like all her former selves. The final bust-in puts her pa in shock, like all the rest. Torn both ways—after all, it is his daughter—he lets the pictures go but runs the film on a continuous roundabout reel, Molly, Dolly, Sally, Holly, Gala, Willa, Sue . . . The reel's still running and the faces lit when we arrive too late to save him or the swiped photos. Unmurder number four . . ."

"So J. Wallington Bradford a.k.a. Tallulah Bankhead cum Crawford cum Colbert is still alive, and he's not a victim?" said Crumley. "The same goes for quick-change artist Quickly?"

"Alive but not for long. They're as flimsy as kites in a long storm. Constance ranted at them—"

"Because?" said Crumley.

"They taught her all the ways to not be herself," said Fritz, proud of his insight. "Don't do this, do that, don't do that, do this. Richard the Third tells you how to be Lear's daughter, Lady Macbeth, Medea. One size fits all. So she became Electra, Juliet, Lady Godiva, Ophelia, Cleopatra. Bradford said. Rattigan did. Same with Quickly. See Connie run! She had to show up on both their doorsteps to disrobe, junk her lines, burn her notices. Can teachers *un*teach? Constance *demanded*. 'Who is Constance, what is she?' was the essence of her declaration. Being only forward teachers, they didn't know how to teach backward. So, Constance was driven to—"

"The basement dressing rooms," I said. "Snatch the pictures from upstairs, sure, but then wipe out the evidence of her former selves on the mirrors. Scrape, erase, eliminate, name by name, year by year."

I finished and sipped my drink and shut up.

"Is the train in *Murder on the Orient Express* pulling into the station?" said Fritz, lying back full-length like Caesar in his bath.

"Yes."

"Furthermore," said Fritz Wong in his fine Germanic guttural, "are you free to accept work on a screenplay titled *The Many Deaths of Rattigan,* starting Monday, five hundred a week, ten weeks, twenty thousand bonus if we finally shoot the goddamn film?"

"Take the money and run," said Henry.

"Crumley, you want me to take his offer?" I said.

"It's dumb thinking but a great film," said Crumley.

"You don't *believe* me?" I cried.

"Nobody could be as nuts as you just said," said Crumley.

"Good God, why have I stood here upchucking my guts?" I sank in my chair.

"I don't want to live," I said.

"Yes, you do." Fritz leaned forward, scribbling on a pad.

Five hundred a week was there.

He threw a five-dollar bill on top.

"Your first ten minutes' salary!"

"Then you *almost* believe? No." I pushed the paper away. "Got to be one of you here gets my idea."

"Me," a voice said.

We all looked at Blind Henry.

"Sign the contract," he said, "but make him sign saying he really believes *every* word you say!"

I hesitated, then scribbled my own manifesto.

Rumbling, Fritz signed.

"That Constance," he growled. "Damn! She shows up at

your door, flings herself on you like a goddamn snake. Hell!
Who cares if she kills herself? Why should she run scared of
her own phone books and look up all the stupid people who
led her down the garden path? Would phone books scare
you? Christ, no! There had to be a reason for her setting out
to run, to seek. Motivation. Why, goddammit, why all that
work, to get what? Hold on."

Fritz stopped, his face suddenly pale, then slowly suffus-
ing with color. "No. Yes. No, couldn't be. No. Yes. *Is!*"

"Is what, Fritz?"

"I'm glad I talk to myself," said Fritz. "I'm glad I listen.
Did anyone *hear?*"

"You haven't said, Fritz."

"I'll talk to myself, and you eavesdrop, *ja?*"

"*Ja,*" I said.

Fritz shot me through the heart with one glare. He
doused his irritation with a swallow of his martini and said,
"A month ago, two months, she threw herself across my
desk, with heavy breaths. Was it true, she cried, I was starting some new film? A movie yet nameless? *Ja,* I said. 'Yes,
maybe.' 'And is there a part for me?' she said, on my shoulder, in my lap. 'No, no,' I said. 'Yes, there must be. There
has to be. Tell me, Fritz, what is it?' I should have never told
her. But I did, God help me!"

"What was the film, Fritz?"

"'What I'm planning is beyond you,' I said."

"Yes, but for God's sake, Fritz. Name the film!"

Fritz ignored me, staring through that monocle into the
starry sky, still talking to himself while we eavesdropped.

"'You can't do it,' I said. She wept. 'Please,' she begged. '*Try* me.' I said, 'Constance, it's something you can never be, something you never were.'" Fritz took another swig from his glass. "The Maid of Orleans."

"Joan of Arc!"

"'Oh, my God,' she cried. 'Joan! If it's the only thing I *ever* do, I must do that!'"

Must do that! came the echo.

Joan!

A voice cried in my ears. Rain fell. Water ran.

A dozen lighters took fire and were thrust out toward the sad, weeping woman.

"Only for my voices, I would lose all heart! The bells came down from heaven and their echoes linger in the fields. Through the quiet of the countryside, my voices!"

The subterranean audience gasped with: Joan.

Joan of Arc.

"Ohmigod, Fritz," I cried. "Say that again!"

"Saint Joan?"

I leaped back, my chair fell.

Fritz went on: "I said, 'Constance, it's too late.' She said, 'It's never too late.' And I said, 'Listen, I'll give you a test. If you pass, if you can do the scene from Shaw's *Saint Joan* . . . impossible, but if you can, you get the job.' She fell apart. She cried, 'Wait! I'm dying! Wait, I'll be back.' And she ran away."

I said, "Fritz, do you know what you've just said?"

"Gottdammit, yes! *Saint Joan!*"

"Oh, Christ, Fritz, don't you see? We've been thrown off

by what she said to Father Rattigan. 'I've killed, I've murdered! Help me bury them,' she cried. We thought she meant old Rattigan up on Mount Lowe, Queen Califia on Bunker Hill, but no, dammit, she didn't murder them, she was out to get help to murder Constance!"

"How's that again?" said Crumley.

"'Help me kill Constance,' said Constance. Why? For *Joan of Arc!* That's the answer. She *has* to have that role. All this month she's been preparing for it. Isn't that it, Fritz?"

"Just a moment while I take my monocle out and put it back in." Fritz stared at me.

"Fritz, look! She's not right for the part. But there is one way she can be Saint Joan!"

"Dammit to hell, say it!"

"Dammit, Fritz, she had to get away from you, fall back, take a long, hard look at her life. She had to, one by one, kill all her selves, lay all the ghosts, so that when all those Constances were dead, she could come for her test, and maybe, just maybe, land the part. She hasn't had a role like that ever in her life. This was her big chance. And the only way she could do it was to *kill the past.* Don't you see, Fritz? That must be the answer to what's been going on during the last week, with all these people, with Constance appearing, disappearing, and reappearing again."

Fritz said, "No, no!"

I said, "Yes, yes. The answer's been lying right in front of us, but it's only when you said the name. Saint Joan is the motive for every woman who ever lived. Impossible dream. Can't be attained."

"I'll be gottdammed."

"Oh, no, Fritz!" I said. "Blessed! You've solved it! Now, if we find Constance and say to her, maybe, just maybe, she has a chance. Maybe, maybe—" I broke off. "Fritz," I said. "Answer me."

"What?"

"If Constance should suddenly appear as the Maid of Orleans, if she were incredibly young, changed in some strange way, would you give her the job?"

Fritz scowled. "Don't push me, dammit!"

I said, "I'm not. Look. Was there ever a time when she could have played the Maid?"

"Yes," he said after a moment. "But that was then and this is now!"

"Hear me out. What if, by some miracle, she should show up? When you think of her, just standing there, don't think of her past at all. When you remember the woman you once knew, if she asked, would you give her the role?"

Fritz pondered, took his glass, downed it, refilled it from a frosted crystal pitcher, and then said, "God help me, I think I might. Don't press me, don't press!"

"Fritz," I said, "if we could find *that* Constance and she asked you, would you at least consider taking a chance on her?"

"Oh, God," Fritz rumbled. "Jesus! Yes! No! I don't know!"

"Fritz!"

"Don't yell, goddammit! Yes! A qualified yes!"

"Okay! All right! Wonderful! Now, if only—"

My eyes strayed, scanning the length of shore to the distant storm-drain entrance. Too late, I glanced away.

Both Crumley and Fritz had caught the look.

"Junior knows where Medea is, right now," said Crumley.

Yes, God, I thought, I know! But my yell had scared her away!

Fritz focused his monocle on that storm-drain entrance.

"Is that where you came out?" he said.

"No thanks to junior here," said Crumley.

"I rode shotgun," I said guiltily.

"Like hell! Shouldn't have been in that sinkhole to start with. Probably found Rattigan, then lost her again."

Probably! I thought. Oh, God, probably!

"That storm drain," Fritz Wong mused. "Maybe, just maybe, *you* ran the wrong way?"

"I *what?*" I said, stunned.

"Here in crazy Hollywood," said Fritz, "is there not more than one way to go? The storm drains, they head in all directions?"

"South, north, west, and—" I slowed down. "East," I said slowly. It's not easy to say "east" slowly, but I did.

"East!" Fritz cried. "*Ja*, east, east!"

We let our thoughts roam over the hills and down toward Glendale. No one ever went to Glendale, except . . .

If someone was dead.

Fritz Wong twisted his monocle in his fierce right eye and probed the eastern skyline, smiling a wonderfully vicious smile.

"Gottdamn!" he said. "This will make the great finale. No script needed. Shall I tell you where Rattigan is? East! Gone to earth!"

"Gone to *what*?" said Crumley.

"Sly fox, swift cat. Rattigan. Gone to earth. Tired, ashamed of all her lives! Hide them all in one final Cleopatra's carpet, roll them up, deposit them in Eternity's bank. Fade out. Darkness. Plenty of earth there to go to."

He made us wait.

"Forest Lawn," he said.

"Fritz, that's where they *bury* people!"

"Who's directing this?" Fritz said. "You took the wrong turn toward open air, the sea, life. Rattigan headed east. Death called her by all two dozen names. She answered with one voice."

"BS!" said Crumley.

"You're fired," said Fritz.

"I was never hired," said Crumley. "What's next?"

"Go and prove I am *right!*" said Fritz.

"So," said Crumley. "Rattigan climbed down into that storm drain and walked east, or drove, or was *driven* east?"

"That," said Fritz, "is how I would shoot it. Film! Delicious!"

"But why would she go to Forest Lawn?" I protested weakly, thinking perhaps I had sent her there.

"To die!" said Fritz triumphantly. "Go read Ludwig Bemelmans' tale of the old man, dead, put a lit candle on his head, hung flowers around his neck, and walked, a one-man funeral, to his own grave! Constance, she does the same. She's gone to die a last time, yes? Now, do I put my car in gear? Will someone follow? And do we go aboveground or take the storm drain direct?"

I looked at Crumley, he looked at me, and we both looked at Blind Henry. He felt our gaze, nodded.

Fritz was already gone, the vodka with him.

"Lead the way," said Henry. "Swear a little now and then to give me direction."

Crumley and I headed for Crumley's old jalopy, Henry in our wake.

Fritz, in his car ahead, banged his motor, blew his horn.

"Okay, you damn Kraut!" cried Crumley.

He thrummed his engine, exploding.

"Which way to the nearest road rage, dammit?"

We paused by the storm drain, stared in, then out at the open road.

"Which is it, smart-ass?" said Crumley. "Dante's Inferno or Route 66?"

"Let me think," I said.

"Oh, *no* you don't!" Crumley cried.

Fritz was gone. We looked along the beach and couldn't see his car anywhere.

We looked to our right. There, speeding off down the tunnel, were two red lights. "Christ!" Crumley yelled. "He's heading in on the flood channel! Damned fool!"

"What are we going to do?" I said.

"Nothing," cried Crumley. "Just this!" He rammed the gas. We swerved and plunged into the tunnel.

"Madness!" I cried.

"Damn tootin'," said Crumley. "Goddamn!"

"I'm glad I can't see this," Henry said from the backseat, speaking to the wind in his face.

We raced up the flood channel, heading inland.

"Can we do it?" I cried. "How high is the flood channel?"

"Most places it's ten feet high," Crumley shouted. "The farther in we get, the higher the ceilings. Floods come down the mountains in Glendale, then the channel has to be really big to take the flood. Hold on!"

Ahead of us, Fritz's car had almost vanished. "Idiot!" I said. "Does he really know where he's going?"

"Yes!" said Crumley. "All the way to Grauman's Chinese then left to the goddamn marble orchard."

The sound of our motor was shattering. In that thunder we saw ahead of us a tide of those lunatics who had assaulted me. "My God," I cried. "We'll hit them! Don't slow down! Those crazies! Keep going!"

We raced along the channel. Our engine roared. The history of L.A. streamed past us on the walls: pictographs, graffiti, crazed illustrations left by wandering homeless in 1940, 1930, 1925, faces and images of terrible things and nothing alive.

Crumley floored the gas. We plunged at the crazed underground mob who shrieked and screamed a horrible welcome. But Crumley didn't slow. We cut through them, tossed them aside.

One ghost rose up flailing, gibbering.

Ed, Edward, Eddie, oh Eduardo! I thought. Is that you?

"You never said good-bye!" the ghost raved and fell away.

I wept and we raced on, outpacing my guilt. We left all behind and the farther we went, the more terrified I became.

"How in hell do we know where we are?" I said. "There aren't any directions down here. Or we can't see them."

Crumley said, "I think that maybe, yeah, let's see." For there were signs on the walls, scribbled in chalk, some in black painted letters.

Crumley slowed the car. On the wall ahead of us someone had etched a bunch of crucifixes and cartoon tombstones.

Crumley said, "If Fritz is any guide, we're in Glendale."

"That means . . ." I said.

"Yeah," he said. "Forest Lawn."

He put on his high beams and swerved the car right and left as we moved slowly, and we saw a ladder leading up to a grate covered by a manhole in the tunnel ceiling and Fritz's car beneath it, and him out of the car and climbing the ladder. A series of crosses ran alongside the ladder leading up.

We got out of the car and crossed the dry wash and began to climb the ladder. There was a thundering clang above us. We saw Fritz's shape and the manhole shoved aside, and the beginnings of a gentle rain pelting his shoulders.

We climbed the ladder in silence. Above us, Fritz was directing and shouting. "Get the hell up here, you damn fools!"

We looked down.

Blind Henry was not about to be left behind.

CHAPTER FORTY-FOUR

THE storm was over but the drizzle stayed. The sky was a loon sky—promising much, delivering little.

"Are we there yet?" said Henry.

We all looked in the gates at Forest Lawn Cemetery, a sweeping hillside covered with a cannonade of memorial stones embedded like meteors in its grass.

"They say that place," said Crumley, "has a greater voting population than Paducah, Kentucky, Red River, Wyoming, or East End, Azusa."

"I like old-fashioned graveyards," said Henry. "Things you can run your hands over. Tombs you can lie on like statues or bring your lady in late hours to play doctor."

"Anyone ever gone in just to check the boy *David's* fig leaf?" said Fritz.

"I hear tell," said Henry, "when they shipped him over,

there was no leaf, so he lay around the north forty a year, under canvas, so old ladies in tennis shoes wouldn't be offended. Day before the fig leaf was glued on to spoil the fun, they had to beat off a gloveless Braille Institute convention. Live folks doing gymnastics in midnight graveyards is called foreplay. Dead folks doing the same is afterplay."

We stood there in the drizzle looking across the way to the mortuary offices.

"Gone to earth," I heard someone murmur. Me.

"Move!" said Crumley. "In thirty minutes the rain from the hills hits below. The flood will wash our cars down to the sea."

We stared at the gaping manhole. We could hear the creek whispering below.

"My God!" said Fritz. "My classic car!"

"Move!" said Crumley.

We ducked across the street and into the mortuary building.

"Who do we ask?" I said. "And *what* do we ask?"

There was a moment of colliding looks, pure confusion. "Do we ask for Constance?" I said.

"Talk sense," said Crumley. "We ask about all those newspaper headlines and names. All those lipstick aliases on the basement dressing-room mirrors."

"Say again," said Henry.

"I'm talking pure circumstantial metaphor," said Crumley. "Double time!"

We double-timed it into the vast halls of death, or to put it another way, the land of clerks and file cabinets.

We did not have to take a number and wait, for a very tall man with ice-blond hair and an oyster complexion glided to the front desk and disdained us as if we were discards from a steam laundry.

He laid a card on the desktop and dared Crumley to take it. "You Grey?" he said.

"Elihu Phillips Grey, as you see."

"We're here to buy gravesites and plots."

A late-winter smile appeared on Elihu P. Grey's mouth and hung there, like a mist. With a magician's gesture, he manifested a chart and price sheet.

Crumley ignored it. "First, I got a list."

He pulled out all the names I had put together but placed it upside down in front of Grey, who scanned the list in silence.

So Crumley pulled forth a rolled wad of one-hundred-dollar bills.

"Hold that, will you, junior?" he said, tossing the wad to me. And then, to Grey: "You know those names?"

"I know all the names." Grey relapsed into silence.

Crumley swore under his breath. "Recite them, junior."

I recited the names, one by one.

"Holly Morgan."

Grey flicked through his file.

"She's here. Buried 1924."

"Polly Starr?"

Another quick run-through.

"Here. 1926."

"How about Molly Circe?"

"Right. 1927."

"Emily Danse?"

"1928."

"All buried here, for sure?"

Grey looked sour. "I have never once in all my life been wrong. Strange, however." He rescanned the items he had drawn out of the file. "Odd. Are they all related, all one *family?*"

"How do you mean?"

Grey fixed his arctic stare at the names. "Because, see here, they're all entombed in the same aboveground Gothic stone hut."

"How's that again?" Crumley lurched from his boredom and grabbed the file cards. "What?"

"Odd, all those different surnames, put to rest in one tomb, a memorial dwelling with eight shelves for eight family members."

"But they *aren't* family!" said Fritz.

"Odd," said Grey. "Strange."

I stood as if struck by lightning.

"Hold on," I whispered.

Fritz and Crumley and Henry turned to me.

Grey lifted his snowy eyebrows. "Ye-e-ss." He made two long syllables out of it. "Well?"

"The tomb house? The family vault? There must be a name on the portico. The name chiseled in marble?"

Grey scanned his cards, making us wait.

"Rattigan," he said.

"Are you sure?"

"I have never—"

"Yes, I know! The name again!"

We all held our breath.

"Rattigan." His cold voice issued from a steel-trap mouth.

We let our air out.

At last I said, "They can't all be there in that one vault."

Grey shut his eyes. "I—"

"I know, I know," I said quickly. I stared at my friends.

"Are you thinking what I'm thinking?"

"Jesus Christ," murmured Crumley. "Goddamn. Can you give us directions to the Rattigan tomb?"

Grey scribbled on a notepad map. "Easy to find. There're fresh flowers out front. The tomb door is open. There will be a memorial service there tomorrow."

"Who's being entombed?"

We all waited, eyes shut, guessing the answer.

"Rattigan," said Grey, almost smiling. "Someone named Constance Rattigan."

CHAPTER FORTY-FIVE

THE rain was so thick the graveyard disappeared. All we could see as we drove uphill in an electric runabout were monuments on the side of the road. The path ahead vanished in the downpour. I carried a map on my lap, marked with an arrow and the name of the area. We stopped.

"It's there," said Crumley. "Azalia Gardens? Plot sixteen. Neo-Palladian edifice."

The rain blew back like a curtain and a flicker of lightning showed us a slender tomb with Palladian pillars on each side of a tall metal door, which stood ajar.

"So if she wants out," said Henry, "she's out. Or invite folks in. Rattigan!"

The rain lifted and blew away and the tomb waited while thunder ran along the far brim of the graveyard. The open door trembled.

Crumley spoke almost to himself: "Jesus! Constance buried herself. Name after name. Year after year. When she was done with one act, one face, one mask, she hired a tomb and stashed herself away. And now, to get the job, maybe, from Fritz, she's killing all her selves again. Don't go in there, Willie."

"She's in there now," I said.

"Horse apples," said Crumley. "Goddamn intuition?"

"No." I shivered. "Goddamn hunch. She's got to be saved." I climbed out.

"She's dead!"

"I'll save her *anyway.*"

"Like hell you will!" said Crumley. "You're under arrest! Get back in here!"

"You're the law, sure, but you're my friend."

I was flooded with cold rain.

"Dammit, dammit all to hell. Go on! Run, you stupid idiot! We'll be waiting downhill. I'll be goddamned if I'll sit and watch your head come flying out that goddamn door. Come find us! Damn you!"

"Hold on!" Fritz cried.

"Hold goddamn nothing!"

Fritz threw a small flask that hit me in the chest.

I stood shivering in the cold downpour and gave Fritz a long look as Crumley, cursing, got out of the runabout slowly. We stood in the big mortuary field with an open iron gate and open tomb door and the rain threatening to wash the bodies out of the earth. I shut my eyes and drank the vodka.

"Ready or not," I whispered. "Here goes."

"Goddammit," said Crumley.

CHAPTER FORTY-SIX

It was a dark and stormy night.

My God, I thought, again?

Feet running. A cry. Lightning, thunder, a few nights back.

And here, my God, the same again!

The gates of heaven burst, a flood poured in darkness, with me near a cold tomb with someone crazed and maybe dead deep in the dark.

Stop, I told myself.

Touch.

The outer gate creaked. The inner door squealed.

We stood in the entry of the marble tomb with the sun gone, never to return, and the rain to rain forever.

It was dark, but there were three small blue votive candles lit and wavering in the draft from the door.

We all looked at the sarcophagus down below on our right.

Holly's name was there. But there was no lid on the sarcophagus and it was empty, save for a powdering of dust.

Our eyes looked up to the next shelf.

Lightning flickered outside in the rain. Thunder mumbled.

On the next shelf Molly's name was cut in marble. But again no lid, and the sarcophagus was empty.

Rain drenched the open door behind us as we looked at the next-to-top and topmost shelves and marble cases. We saw the names of Emily and Polly. We could see one was unoccupied. Trembling, I reached up to probe the top casement. My fingers touched only empty air.

Holly, Polly, Molly, and Emily, but in the flickers of lightning no bodies, no remains.

I stared up at that final enclosure and began to reach up when there was the faintest gasp and something like a cold weeping, far away.

I took my hand down and looked at Crumley. He looked up at the last sarcophagus and at last said, "Junior, it's all yours." There was a final intake of breath above in the shadows.

"Okay," said Crumley, "everyone out."

Everyone backed out into the whispering rain. At the door Crumley looked back at his lunatic child, handed me a flashlight, nodded good luck, and was gone.

I was alone.

I pulled back. The flashlight fell. I almost collapsed. It

took a long while before I found and raised its beam, my heartbeat quaked with it.

"You," I whispered, "there."

Jesus, what did *that* mean?

"It's," I whispered, "me."

Louder.

"I came to find you," I whispered.

"So?" the shadow murmured. The rain behind me fell in a solid sheet. Lightning shimmered. But still no thunder.

"Constance," I said at last to the dark shape on the tall shelf with the shadows of rain curtaining it. "Listen."

And at last I said my name.

Silence.

I spoke again.

Oh God, I thought, she's really dead!

No more of this! Get out, damn, go! But even in turning, the slightest shrug, it happened. The shadow above with a faceless face quickened with the merest breath.

I hardly heard, I only sensed the shadow.

"What?" it exhaled.

I quickened, glad for life, any life, any pulse.

"My name." I gave it again.

"Oh," someone murmured.

Which hammered me to quicker life. I leaned away from rain into cold tomb air.

"I've come to save you," I whispered.

"So?" the voice murmured.

It was the merest mosquito dance in the air, not heard, no, not there. How could a dead woman speak?

"Good," the whisper said. "Night."

"Don't sleep!" I cried. "Sleep and you won't come back! Don't die."

"Why?" came the murmur.

"Because," I gasped. "Because. I say so."

"Say." A sigh.

Jesus, I thought, say *something!*

"Say!" said the faintest shadow.

"Come out!" I murmured. "This isn't your place!"

"Yes." The faintest brush of sound.

"No!" I cried.

"Mine," came the breath in the shadow.

"I'll help you get away," I said.

"From what?" the shadow said. And then, in terrible fear: "Gone. They are gone!"

"They?"

"Gone? They've *got* to be! *Are* they?"

Lightning struck the dark acres at last, thunder knocked the tomb. I spun to stare out at the meadows of stone, the hills of shining slabs with names being sluiced away. And the slabs and stones were lit by the fires in the sky and became names on mirror glass, photos on walls, inked names on papers, and again mirror names and dates being washed away down a storm drain while the pictures fell from the walls and the film slithered through the projector to dance faces on a silver screen ten thousand miles below. Pictures, mirrors, films. Films, mirrors, pictures. Names, dates, names.

"Are they still there?" said the shadow on the top shelf of the tomb.

"Out there in the rain?"

I looked out at the long hill of the mortuary place. The rain was falling on a dozen and a hundred and a thousand stones.

"They mustn't be there," she said. "I thought they were gone forever. But then they began to knock at the door, wake me. I swam out to my friends, the seals. But no matter how far I swam, they were waiting for me on the shore. The whisperers who want to remember what I want to forget."

She hesitated. "So if I couldn't outrun them, I'd have to kill them one by one, one by one. Who were they? Me? So I chased them instead of them me, and one by one I found where they were buried and buried them again. 1925, then 1928, 1930, '35. Where they would stay forever. Now it's time to lie down and sleep forever, or they might call me again at three in the morning. So, where am I?"

The rain fell outside the crypt. There was a long moment of silence and I said, "You're here, Constance, and I'm here, listening."

After a while she said, "Are they all gone, is the shore clear now, can I swim back in and not be afraid?"

I said, "Yes, Constance, they're really buried. You did the job. Someone had to forgive you, that someone had to be Constance. Come out."

"Why?" said the voice from the top shelf of the tomb.

"Because," I said, "this is all crazy, but you're needed. So, please, rest for a moment, and then put your hand out and let me help you down. Do you hear me, Constance?"

The sky went dark. The fires died. The rain fell, erasing the stones and slabs and the names, the names, the terrible names cut to last but dissolving in grass.

"*Are* they?" came the frantic whisper.

And I said, my eyes filled with cold rain, "Yes."

"Yes?"

"Yes," I said. "The yard's empty. The picture's dropped. The mirrors are clean. Now there's only you and me."

The rain washed the unseen stones sinking deep in the flooded grass.

"Come out," I said quietly.

Rain fell. Water slid on the road. The monuments, stones, slabs, and names were lost.

"Constance, one final thing."

"What?" she whispered.

After a long pause I said, "Fritz Wong is waiting. The screenplay is finished. The sets are built and ready."

I shut my eyes and agonized to remember.

Then, at last, I remembered: " 'Only for my voices, I would lose all heart.' "

I hesitated, then continued: " 'It is in the bells I hear my voices. The bells come down from heaven and the echoes linger. In the quiet of the countryside, my voices are there. Without them I would lose heart.' "

Silence.

A shadow moved. A white shape motioned.

The tips of her fingers came out into the shadows and then her hand and then the slender arm.

Then, after a long silence, a deep breath, an exhalation, Constance said: "I'm coming down."

CHAPTER FORTY-SEVEN

THE storm was gone. It was as if it had never been. The sky was clean, not a cloud anywhere, and a fresh breeze was blowing as if to clean a slate, or a mirror, or a mind.

I stood on the beach in front of Rattigan's Arabian fort with Crumley and Henry, mostly silent, and Fritz Wong surveying the scene for long shots and close-ups.

Inside the house two men in white coveralls moved like shadows and I was put in mind of altar attendants somehow, the mind of a crazed writer freely associating, and I wished that somehow, wild as it seemed, Father Rattigan could be there, could be one of those white figures cleaning the house with a censer of incense and a rain of holy water, to re-sanctify a place that had probably never been anywhere near sanctified. Good God, I thought, bring a priest to cleanse a den of iniquity! The housepainters, inside, scraping the walls clean in order to apply fresh paint, worked steadily, not knowing whose house it was and what had lived there. Outside on a table by the pool were some beers for Crumley, Fritz, Henry, and myself, and vodka, if our mood changed.

The smell of fresh paint was invigorating; it promised a lunatic redemption, and an echo of forgiveness. New paint, new life? Please, God.

"How far out does she go?" Crumley stared at the breakers a hundred yards off shore.

"Don't ask me," said Henry.

"Out with the seals," I said, "or sometimes in close. She has a lot of friends out there. Hear?"

The seals were barking, louder or softer I couldn't say, I only heard. It was a glad sound to go with the fresh paint in an old house made new.

"Tell the painters when they paint her mailbox," said Fritz, "to leave room for just *one* name, *ja?*"

"Right," said Henry. He cocked his head to one side, and then frowned. "She's been swimming a long time. What if she don't come in?"

"That wouldn't be so bad," I said. "She loves the water offshore."

"Swells after a storm, fine for surfing. Hey! *That* was *loud!*"

The kind of loud that made for a theatrical entrance.

With superb timing, a cab roared up in the alley behind Rattigan's.

"God!" I said. "I *know* who that is!"

A door slammed. A woman came slogging across the sand that ran between the house and seaside pool, her hands clenched in tight balls. She stood before me like a blast furnace and raised her fists.

"What have you got to say for yourself?" Maggie cried.

"Sorry?" I bleated.

"Sorry!"

She hauled off and struck me a terrible blow on the nose.

"Hit him again," Crumley suggested.

"Once more for luck," offered Fritz.

"What's going *on?*" said Henry.

"Bastard!"

"I know."

"Son of a bitch!"

"Yes," I said.

She struck a second time.

The blood gushed. It flooded my chin and drenched my upraised hands. Maggie pulled back.

"Oh, God," she cried, "what have I done!"

"Hit a son of a bitch and bastard," Fritz answered.

"Right," said Crumley.

"You keep *out* of this!" Maggie yelled. "Someone get a Band-Aid."

I looked at the bright flow on my hands. "Band-Aids won't work."

"Shut up, you stupid womanizer!"

"Only *one,*" I bleated.

"Hold still!" she cried, and raised her fist again.

I held still and she collapsed.

"No, no, enough, enough," she wept. "Oh God, this is terrible."

"Go ahead, I deserve it," I said.

"Do you, *do* you?"

"Yeah," I said.

Maggie glared at the far surf. "Where is she? Out there?"

"Somewhere."

"I hope she never comes in!"

"Me, too."

"What in hell does that mean?"

"I don't know," I said as quietly as possible. "Maybe she belongs out there. Maybe she has friends, dumb friends, and maybe she should stay with them and never come in again."

"If she does, I'll kill her."

"Then she's better off staying way out."

"Are you defending her, damn you?"

"No, just saying she should never have come in. She was always happier on days like this, after a storm, when the waves are right and the clouds are gone. I saw her a few times like that. She didn't drink all day, just kept going out, and there was always the promise she wouldn't come back."

"What got into you? What got into *her?*"

"Nobody knows. It happens all the time. No alibis. It's just things happen, and next thing you know it's all gone to hell."

"Keep talking, maybe you'll make sense."

"No, the more talk the less sense. She was lost for a long time. Now, maybe, she's found. A lot of bull, a lot of malarkey, I don't know. I promised her if she swam out with all those names, she might swim back in as just one. Promises, promises. We'll know when she comes ashore."

"Shut up. You know I love you, don't you, you dumb bastard?"

"I know."

"In spite of all this, you rat, I still love you, God help me. Is this what all women put up with?"

"Most," I said. "Most. No explanations. No reason. Awful truths. The dog wanders. The dog comes home. The dog smiles. You hit him. He forgives you for forgiving him. And it's back home to the kennel or a lonely life. I don't want a lonely life. Do *you?*"

"Jesus help me, no I don't. Wipe your nose."

I wiped it. More blood.

"I'm sorry," she cried.

"Don't be. That's the last thing for you to be. Don't."

"Hold it!" said Henry. "Listen."

"What?" said everyone at once.

"Feel it?" said Henry.

"What, what, dammit?"

"The big surf, the biggest wave, coming in, now," murmured Henry. "And bringing something with it."

Way out, the seals barked.

Way out, a huge wave curled.

Crumley, Fritz, Henry, Maggie, and I held our breath.

And the wave came in.